## "Has It Occurred To You That You're Working On The Wrong Side, Ms. Hancock?"

Jack leaned back in his chair with easy grace. Marisa noticed that his eyes were an intriguing amber, the color of fine sherry or very old, very expensive scotch. *Be careful, Marisa,* she thought.

"I am here to represent my client to the best of my ability, and that I intend to do," she replied evenly. "It would be unprofessional and unethical of me to do anything other than my level best to win this case."

"I see," Jack said. "I'm going to be frank with you. There's much more at stake here than you think."

"I'm aware of that."

"You're at the center of this whirlpool. Do you realize this could be risky for you?"

Marisa met his gaze levelly. "Are you threatening me, Mr. Bluewolf?"

"You've got me wrong," he said huskily. "I was only trying to warn you to be careful...."

Dear Reader,

November is a time for giving thanks, and this year I have an awful lot to be thankful for—my family, my friends and my terrific job. Because it's through my job that I get to bring to you, the readers, books written by fabulous authors. These are love stories that will give you a lift when you're down, that will make you laugh and cry and rediscover the unique joy of falling in love.

This November has so *many* wonderful stories, starting with the latest in Annette Broadrick's SONS OF TEXAS series, *Marriage Texas Style!* (If you missed the earlier SONS OF TEXAS, don't worry, because this volume also stands alone.)

Next, there's our *Man of the Month* ex-sky jockey Kyle Gordon. Kyle is cocky, opinionated, sexy—altogether he's perfect, and he more than meets his match in schoolteacher Susan Brooks.

November is completed with Barbara Boswell's *Double Trouble* (don't ask me to explain the plot—just read the book), Joan Johnston's *Honey and the Hired Hand,* Doreen Owens Malek's *Arrow in the Snow* (welcome back, Doreen!), and Leslie Davis Guccione's *A Rock and a Hard Place.*

So take time from your busy holiday schedule to curl up with a good Desire book. I know I'm going to!

All the best,

Lucia Macro
Senior Editor

# DOREEN OWENS MALEK

## ARROW IN THE SNOW

**SILHOUETTE** *Desire*®
Published by Silhouette Books New York
**America's Publisher of Contemporary Romance**

SILHOUETTE BOOKS
300 East 42nd St., New York, N.Y. 10017

ARROW IN THE SNOW

ISBN: 0-373-05747-4

First Silhouette Books printing November 1992

## DOREEN OWENS MALEK

is a former attorney who decided on her current career when she sold her fledgling novel to the first editor who read it. Since then, she has gained recognition for her writing, winning honors from *Romantic Times* magazine and the coveted Golden Medallion award. She has traveled extensively throughout Europe, but it was in her home state of New Jersey that she met and married her college sweetheart. They now live in their home in Pennsylvania.

# One

**T**he dark man was watching her again.

Marisa Hancock squared off her stack of notes and fastened the pages neatly on the clipboard before her, ignoring the intense gaze focused on her. Staring at the opposition's table in order to unnerve their attorney was an old lawyer's trick and she wasn't going to fall for it. She turned slightly sideways so she wouldn't have to see him and concentrated on the task at hand.

They were deep into the third week of arguments and things were not going well for Marisa. A property and lands grants attorney retained for the case by the federal government, she had taken over from another lawyer at the last minute and found herself plunged into a controversy for which she was not prepared.

Outside the windows the mild sun of a Florida winter shone down on the pale green leaves of trees barely visible through the beveled glass. She knew that the

protesters were still lined up along the sidewalk outside, flanking the impatiens beds with their signs, but
their chanting was not audible from the fourth floor
courtroom. Marisa sighed and tried to concentrate on
the droning of the court clerk's voice, but she still felt
the keen gaze on her face and, yielding to impulse, she
turned and confronted the man who was staring at her.

He gazed back at her, unperturbed. She knew his
name, of course: Jackson Bluewolf, the founder and
president of Natives for Nature, a coalition of native
Americans fighting for conservationist issues, especially the preservation of American Indian shrines and
cultural sites. Bluewolf and his group were in Florida
trying to block the federal takeover of an ancient Seminole burial ground. The government wanted the land
to connect two sections of an interstate highway, and
the Indians wished to keep it and open a museum and
cultural bookstore on the site.

"Ms. Hancock, do you have anything to add to your
argument before I rule on your motion for summary
judgment?" Judge Lasky said briskly, interrupting her
reverie.

"Yes, your honor," Marisa replied, rising from her
seat. "I would remind the court that the savings to the
taxpayers of this state if the government's plan is im-
plemented would be substantial—in the neighborhood
of eight million dollars."

"Thank you, Ms. Hancock. I have given due con-
sideration to your motion and I now rule that it is de-
nied."

Marisa returned to her seat, keeping her face ex-
pressionless, feeling the heat of Bluewolf's gaze on her
back. The two forces had been squaring off for almost
a month, and during that time Bluewolf had not said a

word to her. He merely watched her with his peculiar intensity, and it was making her very ill at ease. Her discomfort was increased dramatically by the growing conviction that she was representing the wrong side.

Bluewolf's group wanted to prevent the government from exercising its rights under "eminent domain"—a doctrine permitting the takeover of any land deemed necessary to further the public interest. Marisa had flown south from her home and practice in Maine to handle the case when another lawyer in her firm was forced to bow out. When she showed up for the preliminary hearing at the last minute she had to fight her way through a crowd of protesters outside the courthouse. Bluewolf had noticed her distress and cleared a path for her, unaware that she would be his adversary. And since that moment it seemed he had never taken his eyes from her.

Marisa had resigned herself to a long stay in Florida when she lost round one and the injunction to halt the highway was granted. Her explanation that the government had no desire to destroy a cultural site but merely wanted to save taxpayers money had carried no weight with the judge. It would cost a fortune to go around the cemetery rather than through it. She had outlined in detail the government's plan to make monetary reparation to the tribe, but it all went for naught. The NFN's argument that money could not make up for the loss of history and tradition that would result from the destruction of the three-hundred-year-old burial ground had carried the day. And Marisa knew that Jackson Bluewolf, the NFN lawyer's chief adviser, had been its architect.

Now she had the almost impossible task of convincing the judge to remove the injunction and let the construction begin. It would be an uphill battle and, like it or not, she was committed to it. She, too, thought that the Indians should be allowed to keep their land, but she could never reveal her feelings. Professional ethics required that she represent her client to the best of her ability, and she was fully prepared to do so.

"Ms. Hancock?" Marisa looked up at the judge, then rose, clearing her throat.

"Are you prepared to continue?"

"Yes, your honor." Marisa said firmly. Then she gathered her papers and put them into her briefcase.

Bluewolf's gaze never wavered as she crossed diagonally in front of his table on her way out of the courtroom.

Several days later, Jackson Bluewolf watched Marisa as she spoke clearly and logically, her arguments cogent and well prepared, as always. It wasn't her fault that local sympathy, among the populace and in the media, was heavily in favor of the Seminoles, or that any lawyer representing the government in the lower courts had a Herculean task from the start. She was losing on points day after day, but she was doing a hell of a job and he had to admire her for it.

He'd been aware of her from day one, mostly because of her looks; she was exactly the sort of tall, slender blonde who usually caught his eye. It had come as something of a shock that she was the attorney for the other side, but her behavior throughout the trial had only made her more attractive to him, despite the fact that she was gunning for the government. She never lost her composure, never betrayed disappointment even when the calls went against her, as they frequently had. And she acted as though she didn't know he existed, which intrigued him. Maybe she didn't, maybe she was so focused on her job that his almost palpable interest in her had failed to register. Well, he was going to find out shortly. In fact, today.

He watched her now, dressed in a tailored navy suit with an ivory silk-tie blouse. Her high-heeled shoes were polished, her pale hair was confined in a stylish chignon, her gold knot earrings matched a gleaming brooch on the lapel of her jacket. She was always like that, tightly controlled, neat as a pin and as finished as a dressmaker's hem. Oh, how he longed to mess her up, to see that shining hair falling loose on creamy, naked shoulders, those lady lawyer clothes piled in an irreverent heap on the floor. His floor. He suddenly realized what he was thinking, swallowed hard, and tore his gaze away from her.

This would never do. When he was in the courtroom he had to concentrate on the case. There would be time enough to pursue her when the session was over for the day.

He could wait no longer.

Marisa was walking down the marble-floored corridor of the courthouse that afternoon on her way back to her hotel when she heard a man call her name.

She knew who it was before she looked. She took a deep breath and then turned and faced him, her expression calm.

"Jackson Bluewolf," he said, extending his hand.

"I know who you are, Mr. Bluewolf," Marisa said dryly, grasping his fingers briefly.

"I wonder if I might speak with you."

"Go on," Marisa replied evenly, looking up at him, thinking that he must be very tall. She was wearing heels and he still topped her by several inches.

"Not here," he said. "Where are you staying?"

Marisa hesitated.

"I merely thought we could have a drink in the lounge," he said mildly, his lips curving slightly.

"At the Fillmore," Marisa said, feeling foolish.

"Good. There's a comfortable bar on the lower level. May I walk you over there?"

"Why?"

"I want to talk to you. Concerning the case, of course."

"I think we're covering everything we need to say in the courtroom," Marisa said.

"It will just take a few minutes. Please."

"All right," Marisa said reluctantly.

He fell into step beside her, saying, "May I take that for you?" He indicated her briefcase.

"I'm used to carrying a bag, Mr. Bluewolf," Marisa said.

"Call me Jack," he said, and smiled.

Be careful, Marisa, she thought. At close range his charm was overwhelming, a combination of his arresting good looks, his physical grace, and the easy smile which revealed beautiful, slightly uneven white teeth. He was wearing a taupe pinstriped suit which complemented his dusky skin and gleaming black hair. His eyes, she noticed, were not the dull brown of ordinary eyes but an intriguing amber, the color of fine sherry or very old, very expensive Scotch.

Yes, be very careful indeed.

"So what is this about, Mr. Bluewolf?" she said briskly.

He chuckled.

"What?" she said, startled, looking over at him.

"Jack," he reminded her gently.

Marisa shrugged. There was something about him that made standing on ceremony seem ridiculous.

They emerged from the building into the balmy late-afternoon air. The hotel was just across the main street and he took her elbow as they traversed the intersection. Marisa felt herself stiffen and then relaxed deliberately. Really, she was acting like a child.

The hotel bar was thronged with happy hour revelers. Jack greeted the host familiarly and they were shown to a secluded corner, away from the noise and confusion.

"Your friend?" Marisa said, nodding toward the departing man.

Jack made a deprecating gesture. "I've been in Ponte Azul for several months now, working on the case. This place is convenient to the courthouse; Ben and I have been in here quite a bit."

Ben was Ben Brady, the NFN lawyer, and the mention of his name reminded Marisa why she was there.

"Well?" she said.

He raised his brows.

"The case."

"Oh, yeah, the case. I was wondering if it has occurred to you that you're working for the wrong side."

This statement so accurately reflected what she had been thinking that she froze, stunned. She waited for a long moment and then said smoothly, "I'm not going to discuss politics with you, Mr. Bluewolf."

"Politics?"

"The goals of the NFN, while they may be laudable, are a political matter. I am here to represent the federal government to the best of my ability in a court case, and that I intend to do. It would be unprofessional and unethical of me to do anything other than my level best to win the case for my client."

"Well said," Jack observed, watching her face.

A waitress arrived to take their order.

"What will you have?" Jack said, looking at her.

"Club soda with lime."

"And a bourbon for me. Thanks." He waited until the woman had departed and said, "You're a last-minute replacement, aren't you?"

"How did you know that?"

"The papers your firm filed indicated that somebody named Arthur Winston was going to be representing the feds. Then you showed up at the preliminary hearing, and even before I heard the judge address you by name, I would have bet good money you weren't Arthur Winston."

"Arthur was in a car accident and I had to take over when it was clear he wouldn't be able to continue."

"I see." He sat back in his chair and folded his arms. "I'm going to be frank with you, Ms. Hancock. There is much more at stake here than a cemetery or a highway. The Seminoles are using this hearing as a forum to air a long history of unfair treatment by the government. The protesters, the editorials in the local papers, the tempers flaring all over the county have little to do with the court case. They have much more to do with the poor conditions of reservation living which have left all of the Indians in this area bitter and malcontent."

"I'm aware of that," Marisa said evenly.

"You're now at the center of this whirlpool, the most visible representative of the government and therefore identified with its position. Do you realize this could be dangerous for you?''

Marisa met his eyes levelly across the tiny table. ''Are you threatening me, Mr. Bluewolf?'' she said quietly.

His face went blank. His drink came at that moment and he gulped about half of it before he replied.

''You've got me wrong,'' he said huskily. ''I was only trying to warn you to be careful.''

''I'm sure it won't shock you to learn that a warning like that could be viewed as intimidation.''

''You're jumping to the wrong conclusion, Ms. Hancock.''

''Possibly, and if I am, I apologize. I'm merely basing my reaction on my past experiences. You wouldn't be the first person to try scare tactics when I turned out to be a little more formidable than I look. Some threats are more subtle than, 'Catch the next plane out of here, lady, or you'll be sorry.'''

''Do you really think that of me?'' he said softly, holding her gaze deliberately.

''Mr. Bluewolf, I don't know you. I do know that my arrival here was not exactly good news for your organization, and even though my case has not been going well lately each day I keep on fighting. It would be much easier, and cheaper, to drive me out of town than to bear the expense of countering every motion that I file. If I'm terrified into dropping the case, you win. If I'm terrified into leaving it to someone else, the confusion and delay caused by replacing me can only work to your advantage. Am I making my position clear to you?''

''Perfectly,'' he said tightly.

"Good," she said, rising smoothly. "I'm so glad that we understand each other."

He shoved his chair back and stood also, his eyes blazing.

"Thank you for the drink," she said primly, leaving it untouched at her place as she turned and walked away.

Jack drained his glass as he watched her go, then slammed it onto the table so hard it cracked.

Damned impossible woman. She had completely misinterpreted his intentions. But somehow, instead of turning him off, her cool, determined response had only gouged the hook in deeper.

He could hardly wait to see her the next day.

Marisa unlocked the door to her hotel room, feeling very satisfied with herself. Did Bluewolf actually think she would fall for that tired old bullying routine? And even if the man was sincerely concerned for her safety she had shown him that she wasn't going to turn tail and run.

The message light on her telephone was flashing and she called the desk. Charles Wellman, the head of the litigation department at her firm, had called while she was at court.

Marisa looked at her watch. Charlie often worked until six and would probably still be in his office.

"Charles Wellman," he said, after two rings.

"Answering your own phone?" Marisa said teasingly.

"Margaret's left for the day. How's it going down there?"

Marisa sighed heavily.

"That bad?" Charles said glumly.

"Oh, come on, Charlie, you knew what this would be like when you asked me to take Arthur's place. The courthouse is ringed with protesters every day, the editorial page of the local paper is filled with commentary about the big bad feds moving in to destroy a revered cultural site, and the judge is up for reelection next spring. How do you think it should be going?"

"Are you holding your own?"

"I guess so. Judge Lasky even ruled in my favor today. Once."

"Remember what I said. Lean heavily on how much money the taxpayers are going to save if the highway goes through the cemetery."

"I have, I have. But it's a political football, Charlie. Even if there are some people who would rather save the money than the site, nobody is going to say so. Not out loud, not around here. Oh, and I forgot. The head honcho of the NFN asked me to have a drink with him this afternoon and then gave me a nice little speech about how concerned he was for my safety."

"Jackson Bluewater?"

"Wolf. Bluewolf. The very same."

"What's that supposed to mean, 'your safety'? Are you getting hate letters or anything?"

"No, no. I guess it's possible that a few of the protesters could get carried away or something, but I personally think he was just trying to rattle me."

"Did he succeed?"

"Please. You're talking to the woman who went up against Big Jim Lafferty and the United Dock Workers last year. I'm fine."

"What's he like, Bluewolf?"

"About what you'd expect. Lots of teeth and charm. I'm sure he's a very effective spokesperson for his cause, the wattage from his smile alone must be good for quite a few petition signatures.''

''And Ben Brady?''

''The NFN lawyer? Very good, as befits a full partner of Henner, Wilson and Drumm. Did you know they were doing the whole thing *pro bono?* Very good publicity. It's mentioned in the papers about three times every day, how the noble NFN legal team is working for free, along with speculation about the outrageous amount the evil feds are paying us to do their dirty work.''

''Sounds like it's getting to you.''

''It isn't the first time I've been unpopular.''

''Well, anyway, I'm sending you some help.''

''You've resurrected Clarence Darrow?''

''Next best thing. I've arranged for Tracy Carswell to take her exams early so she can fly down there and assist you with the case. She doesn't have to be back at school until the end of January so you'll have her at least until you break for the holidays.''

''Charlie, that's wonderful! I could sure use a research assistant. I'm trying new things practically every day and barely have time to look up the precedents.''

''She's yours. She'll be there tonight. Margaret already booked the room adjoining yours—it opens into a suite.''

''Best news I've had since I got here. Tracy's a terrific intern. Things are looking up, suddenly.''

''Keep the faith, kid. The firm's not expecting miracles, we just have to show the government that we put up a decent fight for them. If the decision goes against you no one will be shocked.''

''Or disappointed?''

"That I can't promise. It would be wonderful if you could pull this one out of the hat."

There was a long silence. Then Marisa said resignedly, "I'll do my best."

"I know you will. I'll be in touch. Take care."

"Goodbye." Marisa hung up the phone just as someone knocked on her door.

"Yes?"

"Delivery," a man's voice said.

Marisa opened the door and was handed a small wicker basket covered with green glassine florist's wrap.

"Are you sure this is for me?" she asked, puzzled.

The delivery man looked down at his manifest. "Marisa Hancock, Room 213?"

"Yes."

"It's for you."

Marisa fumbled in her handbag for a tip and then closed the door. She ripped off the wrapping and saw a small white card nestled in a bed of fragrant local orange blossoms.

"You have misjudged me. Give me another chance," was scrawled in bold handwriting, covering most of the card. It was signed, "Jack."

Typical egotism, Marisa thought. As if he were the only Jack in the world. She lifted the basket to her nose and inhaled the heady, haunting perfume. Then she set the basket on the end table next to the phone and picked up the room service menu to order dinner.

Marisa was reviewing her notes from the day's proceedings when there was a knock at her door followed by Tracy's voice calling, "Yoo-hoo, it's me!"

Marisa pulled the door open to admit Tracy, who was wearing a T-shirt emblazoned with "Welcome to the Sunshine State", and a straw hat decorated with plastic lemons and limes.

"Your research department has arrived," she announced and threw herself full-length on the bed.

"And costumed for the part," Marisa replied, laughing.

"I bought this stuff at the airport. I've never been to Florida and so I thought I'd get into the spirit. Not exactly Maine, is it? At home the temperature was twenty-eight degrees."

"And how are things in Bar Harbor?"

"Frigid. I can't believe old Charlie decided to fly me down here. You must have convinced him it was time to send in the marines."

"We've been talking every day."

"Aha. Well, I can't say that I was depressed to hear that I was about to depart the frozen tundra and arrive in lotus land."

"Don't get too happy. You won't have time for the beach. You'll be working."

"What about weekends?"

"Weekends, too."

"You can't spare Sunday afternoons for two hours? I can't go back without a tan, nobody will believe I was ever here." Tracy rolled over on the bed and spied the flowers on the table. "What's this?"

Marisa made a dive for the basket but Tracy got there first. "Give me another chance," she murmured. "Jack. Who's Jack?"

"Nobody, forget it," Marisa said, snatching the card away.

"Jack, Jack, Jack," Tracy muttered. Her expression brightened. "That's the NFN leader, Jackson something, right? I just saw him on TV last week."

"Coincidence," Marisa said, not too convincingly.

"It is not," Tracy said, grinning. "You've been here three weeks and you've got the head of the opposition team sending you flowers. Why is it these things never happen to me?"

"You're making too much of it. I hardly know the man. He thinks I misunderstood something he said and this was his way of..."

"Courting you?" Tracy supplied.

"Don't be ridiculous. He was trying to apologize, I suppose."

"I suppose you haven't noticed that he's gorgeous."

"Tracy, give me a break. I've been far too busy to ogle anybody at the opposition table."

"Oh, I see. You've been struck blind."

Marisa threw Tracy a look which would have silenced anyone else, but Tracy was more persistent than the average busybody. "So what did you misunderstand?" she inquired.

"Well, he asked me to have a drink with him..."

"Aha!" Tracy said triumphantly, sitting up alertly.

"To warn me that my high profile defense of the federal government's position might be dangerous for me."

"Oh. That was nice of him."

Marisa stared at her.

"What?" Tracy said, turning her hands palms up innocently.

"That was just a little more sophisticated form of intimidation, Tracy. Letting me know, under the guise of concern, that there was definitely something to be worried about."

"Marisa, you're paranoid."

"Am I? Do you know how many times during the Lafferty trial one of those goons took me aside for a little friendly chat, warning me, very nicely and politely, that if I kept on with the case I could wind up in a pair of cement shoes?"

"They actually said that?" Tracy muttered, aghast.

"Of course not. They were more subtle about it, though none quite approached the smoothness of our man Bluewolf. He practically oozed solicitude."

"Maybe he was sincere, Marisa."

Marisa rolled her eyes.

Tracy shook her head. "You've been spending too much time around hoods, prosecuting these federal cases."

"Maybe so. But I'm a little too old to fall for Mr. Bluewolf's practiced charm."

"So he is charming, you admit it."

"If you like the type."

"What type?"

Marisa shrugged.

"The handsome, sophisticated, politically correct type?" Tracy suggested, grinning.

"Shut up, Tracy," Marisa said wearily. "It's time for us to get to work."

"What?" Tracy said, outraged. "I don't even eat dinner first?"

"We'll order you a burger from room service."

"Thanks a lot."

Marisa handed her a manila folder with a computer printout stapled to its cover.

"What's this?" Tracy said, fingering the sheet.

"A list of all the eminent domain cases decided in the state of Florida in the last fifty years."

"Gee, how thoughtful."

"I knew you wouldn't want to waste a minute."

Marisa handed Tracy the phone and pointed to the house extension for room service.

The next morning in court Marisa moved to gain access to the Seminole tribal records detailing the number and location of the graves in the burial site to determine the cost of moving them. She was stunned when Judge Lasky granted the motion, and so was the press corps, which departed en masse for the phones. By the time the morning session ended they were lined up in the corridor, waiting for her comments on a development that was sure to incense the Indian community and provide for some juicy quotes from both sides. She stared through the courtroom doors in dismay at the milling crowd, wishing that she hadn't sent Tracy to the library that morning. She would have appreciated the company.

"I wouldn't go that way if I were you," Jack's voice said behind her.

"It's probably not a good idea for you, either," Marisa replied dryly, turning to look at him. He was wearing a beige lightweight wool suit with a tobacco brown shirt that turned his amber eyes to gold.

"I know a shortcut through the lower level," he said.

Marisa eyed him warily.

"I'm only trying to help," he said innocently.

"Is that so?"

"Through that door," he said, pointing. "You'll avoid the pack of vultures and exit in the parking lot."

Marisa sighed and nodded.

They went to the back of the courtroom and then down a flight of fire stairs, Jack leading the way. They came out into what was obviously a basement, with pipes running overhead and cement floors. As Jack turned toward another door marked "Service," two people Marisa recognized as reporters rounded a bend and headed toward them

"Oh, oh," Jack said.

"I guess you weren't the one only who thought of this brilliant maneuver," Marisa observed.

"They haven't seen us. This way," he said, grabbing her hand.

Marisa didn't have time to protest as he dragged her back the way they had come and into a side corridor, yanking open the first door he saw. They dashed through it and Marisa stepped into a bucket, which clanged loudly.

"This is a broom closet," she said, removing her foot.

"I see that." He pulled the door closed and the motion disturbed a mop stored behind it, which tipped forward and struck him on the head. Marisa covered her mouth with her hand, trying not to laugh.

"So what do you think of my dashing rescue?" he said, removing a mop string from his eye.

"Very impressive," she said, giving way to giggles.

"Hey, did you avoid the reporters, or what?" He replaced the mop in the corner and turned to face her. They stared at each other in the confined space as their smiles faded and the silence lengthened.

"They're probably gone by now," Marisa finally said.

"What?" he said, seemingly dazed.

"I think it's safe to go," she observed.

"Oh. Right." He nodded and reached for the doorknob, stepping back to let Marisa precede him through the door. Once they were back in the hall they looked around cautiously, but the coast was clear.

"I guess we cut those varmints off at the pass," he said dramatically, and she smiled again.

"That's a nice change," he said. "I'm so used to having you glowering at me that I was beginning to wonder if you knew how to smile."

Marisa didn't know what to say.

"Did you get the flowers I sent?" he asked.

"Yes. Thank you."

"I meant what I said on the card." He put his hand on her arm. "My warning was well intentioned. Some of these activist kids can get carried away. They get caught up in situations like this one and lose sight of the big picture."

"What is the big picture?" she asked quietly.

"Well, let's just say that it's not going to do our cause any good to persecute an attorney who's merely representing the opposition in a legal case. Personalities shouldn't enter into it."

"But not everyone in your NFN group sees it quite that way," she said softly.

He shrugged. "They're frustrated and angry because you're doing a good job. Getting the tribal records unsealed was a coup for your side and it's going to cause trouble. Up until now there have been rumblings, but the case has been going against you. They don't want to see it turn the other way, however slightly."

"So will my hotel room be firebombed?" Marisa asked lightly.

"Not if I can help it," he replied huskily.

Marisa realized that he was gripping her wrist tightly. She looked down at his hand and his fingers relaxed, letting her go.

"I have to get to my car," she said hastily. "There are some notes there I need for the afternoon session."

"May I take you to lunch?" he asked, his eyes on her face.

"No, I need the time to prepare. I was going to skip lunch."

He shook his head. "All that dedication. Do you think the feds deserve it?"

"Any client deserves my best representation," she said flatly.

"Oh, don't frost over again, Ms. Hancock. I was teasing. I'll walk you to your car."

They ascended a set of steps from the basement and walked out into the noon sunshine.

"There's my car," Marisa said. "Thank you."

Jack looked at the economy rental and said dryly, "For what the government is paying your firm you'd think they could have sprung for a more luxurious model."

"This is fine for me."

"Simple tastes, eh?"

"Bad driver. Those ritzy cars with the elaborate instrument panels look like you need a pilot's license to drive them. I like the ones that say, 'drive' and 'neutral' and 'reverse.' More than that scares me."

"Now I would have guessed that very little scared you."

"Anything mechanical sends me into a frenzy."

He took the keys from her hand and opened the door for her. Marisa reached into the back seat and extracted her leather overnight bag.

"Here it is," she said.

He saluted.

"See you in court," he said and sauntered away.

# Two

———

"**B**ad news," Tracy said, dropping the morning paper on Marisa's breakfast tray.

"Is there any other kind?" Marisa said wearily.

"Well, today there are two kinds. That headline says there was a brawl last night at one of the downtown bars. It was between a group of the Indian kids and some of the locals who want the government plan to go through for the jobs it will provide. One of the Seminole ringleaders, an eighteen-year-old boy, was killed."

"Oh my God," Marisa whispered, turning pale. The piece of toast she was holding fell to her plate.

"And as if that weren't enough, we've been assigned an 'adviser' by the Bureau of Indian Affairs. A Mr. Randall Block will be arriving sometime tomorrow to aid in the handling of the case. We're to give him our 'fullest cooperation.'" Tracy dropped the message on top of the newspaper and faced Marisa glumly, her hands on her hips.

"Maybe it's good that he's coming, he might be able to give me some advice," Marisa said quietly. "I never counted on anyone being killed, Tracy. This is just awful."

"The paper says it was an accident. It seems the boy got into a shoving match with some guy and when his opponent pushed back the kid fell and hit his head."

"Either way the boy is dead. No highway is worth a human life, for heaven's sake."

Tracy nodded soberly.

"I feel like dumping this case right now."

"The government will only go ahead with somebody else, and you'll be in hot water at the firm," Tracy said. "You might as well stay and see this through."

The telephone rang at Tracy's elbow and she picked it up on the first ring.

"Hello?" She listened for a second and then said, "No, this is her assistant. Just a second, she's right here."

"Who is it?" Marisa asked.

Tracy handed her the phone and said, "Jackson Bluewolf, the man you hardly know."

Marisa threw her a dirty look as she took the phone. "Hello?" she said tentatively.

"Did you hear about what happened last night?" Jack demanded tersely.

"Yes. I'm so dreadfully sorry. I don't know what to say."

"There's nothing to say. I'm calling to tell you to ask the judge for a postponement. I need a few days to get these young turks calmed down. If the hearing goes on as planned today there could be real trouble."

"Lasky already gave my team three continuances when Arthur had his accident. He's not going to want to hear any more on that subject from me. Can't your guy ask him?"

"Brady doesn't *want* to ask him. His thinking is, the more trouble stirred up, the better for our side. And Lasky has made it clear that he wants this over with as soon as possible."

"I can't ask for more time, Judge Lasky will censure me. Brady has to do it."

There was an impatient sound from the other end of the line. "He won't listen to me. He wants to win the case and doesn't care if anybody else gets hurt."

"That's a strange comment coming from you, Mr. Bluewolf. Some people would say your only role in this has been to exacerbate the existing problem," Marisa replied testily.

There was a long silence and then Jack said, "I'm here because I didn't want to see any more Indians robbed of their land by the government, Ms. Hancock. That's all."

"Of course. You're perfectly innocent. You must have heard the story of the sorcerer's apprentice."

"What?" he said, exasperated.

"Don't you remember the story about the trainee magician who was drowned by the waters he summoned? He initially got what he wanted but then lost control of his creation."

The phone slammed down in her ear.

Marisa replaced the receiver carefully.

"What happened?" Tracy asked.

"That man is amazing. He has more gall than any other three people I know. He comes here to rile up the Seminoles and get them on the march, and then when his plan succeeds too well he wants me to help him dampen the fires by asking for a continuance."

"I wouldn't do that," Tracy said warily. "From what you've told me about Lasky, he'll go wild."

"Of course he will. Brady won't do it, mind you, but Bluewolf thinks he can maneuver me into it. Lasky will hang me out to dry, and Bluewolf knows it. But there he is on the phone anyway, not asking, mind you, but demanding that I help him with a problem he created when he knows doing so would hurt *my* case."

"He didn't create the problem, Marisa. The Seminoles were protesting long before he got here."

"He intensified it, then. He isn't even a Seminole, he's a Blackfoot from the Quadro Reservation in Oklahoma! He goes all over the country putting in his two cents for Indian causes, which is fine I suppose, even commendable..."

"But not when it interferes with the progress of your career," Tracy interjected.

"That isn't fair!" Marisa countered, tossing her crumpled breakfast napkin in the trash. "I have no desire to see anyone else get hurt, either. I merely resent the fact that he thinks he's going to pressure me into doing as he says when his own lawyer won't listen to him."

"Aren't you overreacting a little? I guess he figured it was worth a try."

Marisa leaned forward urgently. "If I ask for a delay, Lasky becomes even more prejudiced against me than he already is, Brady is in the clear, and Bluewolf gets what he wants without sacrificing an iota of Lasky's goodwill for his side. Wouldn't you feel used in my place?''

"I suppose so," Tracy said slowly. Then, after a moment, "What are you going to do?"

"If Mr. Bluewolf wants a delay he can ask for it himself. I'll be in court at nine o'clock as planned," Marisa said flatly and went to the bathroom to take a shower.

Marisa's bravado deserted her when she stepped outside the hotel at eight forty-five and saw the mob scene across the street at the courthouse. There seemed to be at least three times the usual number of people assembled outside and the sound level was deafening. As she moved toward the intersection with Tracy at her side, it seemed that the protesters turned as one body to stare at them and, incredibly, the crowd noise got even louder.

"Oh my God," Tracy said at her side. "We should have requested a federal marshal as an escort."

"Don't show them that you're scared," Marisa replied.

"If you wanted a performance like that you should have sent me to acting school," Tracy responded darkly.

They marched, side by side like soldiers, across the street and into the crowd, which parted for them like the Red Sea. Marisa looked straight ahead as they walked up the courthouse steps, so she didn't see the arm emerging from the mob, the arm holding the gun.

What happened next was a blur. She heard Tracy scream and saw Jackson Bluewolf appear before her like a genie out of a bottle. He grabbed her upper arms and thrust her aside so powerfully that she fell. At the same instant she heard the crack of a gunshot and Jack tumbled to the steps nearly on top of her, his shoulder smudged dark with a powder burn and then blossoming red.

The scene was chaos. Marisa struggled to her knees, stunned, as people began running to and fro yelling, "He's hit!" and "Get an ambulance!" Policemen she hadn't seen previously materialized as if from nowhere and subdued the assailant, who was sobbing, "I didn't mean Jack, I didn't mean to shoot Jack!" And Bluewolf was crumpled like a discarded doll on the courthouse steps, his eyes closed, blood staining his jacket and running down his arm.

Marisa crawled over to him and yanked on his tie, loosening his collar. His eyes fluttered open and for a second she was sure he knew her. Then someone appeared at her side saying, "I'm a doctor," and she was pulled away as all attention was directed to the wounded man.

She didn't realize she was crying until Tracy sat down next to her on the steps, oblivious to the crowd milling around them, and handed her a tissue. The clicking and whirring of cameras formed an incessant backdrop to the other noises surrounding them.

"That bullet was meant for me," Marisa gasped.

"I know," Tracy said, not meeting her eyes. "The shooter was the dead boy's brother. I heard somebody talking about it."

They both watched as Jack was loaded onto a stretcher and carried down the steps into a waiting ambulance.

"You don't have to say it," Marisa added dully. "I know it's all my fault."

Tracy just shook her head.

"I want to go after the ambulance to the hospital," Marisa said quickly, rising.

"I doubt if they'll let you in to see him."

"I have to try."

Tracy stood also. "At any rate, we'd better get out of here. Once the excitement dies down we might become very unpopular. Let's go."

They went back to the hotel, where Marisa called the hospital. Bluewolf was listed as stable, whatever that meant, but was allowed no visitors.

"Tracy, you'd better stay here," Marisa said. "See if you can get through to Judge Lasky's chambers, and then get in touch with the firm. Take messages for any calls that come through here."

Tracy stared at her.

"Don't look at me that way."

"You'll just be mobbed at the hospital," Tracy said.

Marisa went there anyway.

The lobby was full of reporters and police. The NFN lawyer, Ben Brady, spotted Marisa and scuttled to her side, grabbing her shoulder and steering her into a side hallway.

"What the hell are you doing here?" he said, looking past her at the room they'd just left.

"Same thing you are," Marisa responded, yanking her arm from his grasp. "I want to make sure Bluewolf is all right."

"If you go back out there the press will eat you alive. It's common knowledge already that the kid was aiming at you."

"And did you aid in disseminating that knowledge?" Marisa inquired coldly.

"Hey, don't blame me for your screwup. If you had asked for the continuance this might not have happened."

"You had the same opportunity to do so that I did! Bluewolf told me he wanted you to talk to Lasky and you refused."

"When did he tell you that?" Brady asked, his eyes narrowing.

"Never mind, it's not important now. Can you get me upstairs to see him or not?"

"Why should I do that?" Brady countered.

"Because he was hurt trying to protect me. A decent person would let me satisfy my conscience that he's all right," Marisa said evenly.

Brady studied her in silence.

"Or am I making an incorrect assumption that you're a decent person?"

Brady shrugged. "I can take you up to his room, but my guess is that's as far as you'll get."

"I'll take that chance."

Brady turned around and guided her through the crowd, shoving off aggressive reporters and ignoring the shrill cries which surrounded them. They were almost running when they reached the elevator. Brady punched the button with the flat of his hand and they fell against the inside walls of the cage as the doors closed and it ascended.

"Nice group, eh?" he said sarcastically.

When they got to the third floor the atmosphere was much calmer, brisk and efficient. Brady introduced Marisa to the attending doctor at the nurse's station.

"How is Mr. Bluewolf?" Marisa said anxiously.

"You're not a relative, right?"

"No, I'm . . ."

"The target of the gunman," Brady finished for her when she hesitated.

"Ah, I see," the doctor said, nodding. "Well, he's lost a lot of blood, but we're transfusing him and he's young and healthy. We'll be operating soon to remove the bullet. Unless he throws a clot or something else extraordinary happens, he should recover from the wound all right."

Marisa closed her eyes. "Thank you."

"Why did that guy take the bullet for you?" the doctor asked her curiously.

"He didn't mean to, it was an accident. He was trying to shove me out of the way," Marisa said.

"Haven't you heard, Doctor?" Brady said lightly. "Chivalry is not dead."

Marisa silenced him with a look.

"May I see him?" she asked the doctor.

The doctor shook his head. "Not until after the surgery. His sister and mother are on their way out from Oklahoma. Once they get here they can determine the visiting list."

"May I wait around until the operation's over?"

He gestured toward a small waiting room at the end of the corridor. "You can sit in there if you want. It will be a while." He hurried off to waylay a passing nurse.

"Are you going to hang around here?" Brady asked Marisa.

"Yes."

"Why don't you go back to your hotel? I'll call you."

Marisa shook her head. "I'll wait."

"Feeling responsible?" he said baitingly.

"Goodbye," Marisa said, turning her back. She walked to the waiting room and sat down in one of the plastic chairs.

It was a very long day. She talked to Tracy on the phone a couple of times, watched a soap opera on the lounge television and then fell asleep. When she woke up it was dark and a nurse was shaking her.

"Aren't you waiting on the Bluewolf case?" she asked.

"Yes," Marisa replied worriedly, sitting up quickly.

"He's out of recovery and back in his room. He'll be fine."

Marisa nodded wordlessly and pressed the nurse's hand.

"Why don't you go home?" the nurse suggested kindly.

Marisa stood stiffly and headed for the hall.

It was stretching a point to call a hotel "home."


"You're not going back to the hospital?" Tracy said in an exasperated tone the next morning. They were in the hotel coffee shop.

"There might have been a change overnight."

"And what if the relatives are there? Do you think they're going to fall on your neck in welcome?"

"I'll deal with them."

"Charlie is supposed to call this morning. That detective from the local police is coming back. He wants you to fill out an incident report on the shooting. And that guy, Block, from the Bureau of Indian Affairs will be here this afternoon. He'll want to see you, not me."

"I'll be back by four," Marisa replied, picking up her purse. "I'll check in with you in a couple of hours.

Lasky may make a decision today about when to resume the hearing.''

"And what if he wants to talk to you directly?"

"Call me at the hospital, third floor lounge."

Tracy threw up her hands and went back to her omelet. If Marisa insisted on keeping this vigil there was nothing she could do about it.

Jack's mother and sister were in the hall outside Jack's room when Marisa got there. They didn't have to be identified. The tall, beautiful girl with waist-length black hair looked just like him and the older woman was obviously her mother.

"I'm Marisa Hancock," Marisa said to the girl, extending her hand, her heart pounding.

The girl looked at her blankly.

"The government's attorney in the highway case," Marisa explained flatly.

The girl's eyes widened. "You're the one Jeff Rivertree was trying to shoot," she said incredulously.

Marisa nodded bleakly.

"What's going on, Ana?" her mother asked, looking from one young woman to the other.

"I'll handle this, Mama," the girl said. "Why don't you go into the lounge and have a seat? I'll be right with you."

The older woman hesitated, then left. Jack's sister turned back to Marisa.

"I'm Ana Carter, Jackson's sister. What are you doing here, Ms. Hancock?" she asked coldly.

"I was hoping to get in to see your brother."

The girl folded her arms and stared back at Marisa, who refused to flinch.

"You want to visit my brother, Ms. Hancock?" she asked, raising her dark brows.

"Well, yes."

"Do you really think he'll want to see you?"

"It's more like I need to confirm for myself that he's all right," Marisa admitted.

"Jack's doctor's word is not good enough for you?"

Marisa sighed and looked down at her hands. "Ms. Carter, this situation is complicated. Suffice it to say that I feel a responsibility for your brother's injury. Isn't that enough reason to be concerned?"

"Yes, I talked to Mr. Brady. I can understand your position, Ms. Hancock, and I would not want to be in it."

Marisa straightened and looked at the other woman directly. "Do I get to see him or not?" she asked baldly.

"Not," Ana Carter replied crisply. "Relatives only today."

"What about tomorrow?"

"That's up to the doctor."

"Fine. I'll be back tomorrow."

Marisa turned to go and Jack's sister called after her, "You'll probably be wasting your time."

"I'll take that chance," Marisa replied. She went around the bend in the corridor as Ana Carter looked after her.

That evening Marisa met with Randall Block from the Bureau. He was concerned only with winning the legal case and irritated her with a number of impractical suggestions designed to inflame the situation even further. After that unproductive experience she went to the police station and answered a lot of obvious questions. When she got back to the hotel she learned that the case had been continued for two weeks, and that her firm had given her permission to remain in Florida to work on it.

"Are you surprised Charlie isn't flying down here to oversee things himself?" Tracy asked. They were both too keyed up to sleep.

"I'm surprised I haven't been recalled to Maine and then shot at sunrise," Marisa replied wearily, stretching out on her bed.

"Are they going to blame you for Bluewolf's injury?" Tracy asked quietly.

"What does it matter? I blame myself."

"Why? Legally, you made the right decision. If Brady wasn't going to risk angering Lasky you had every right to resist doing so yourself. Any attorney would have done the same."

"I didn't make the decision for legal reasons only," Marisa said, closing her eyes.

Tracy sat at the foot of the bed, waiting.

"I said I did, I even convinced myself that I did, but if I'm brutally honest I have to admit there was another element involved." Marisa opened her eyes.

"Well?" Tracy said.

"I'm attracted to Bluewolf, and he knows it. He was trying to use that to manipulate me into doing what he wanted."

"Oh, Marisa, are you sure?"

Marisa put her arm across her forehead. "I haven't been with him that much, but the chemistry was vividly, definitely there. I'm sure he's accustomed to having that effect on women and I didn't want to be just another bimbo he dazzled and then controlled."

"Even so, you made the right move for your client," Tracy said stubbornly. "And I'm sure you would have made the right move for your client anyway, you're too professional to do anything else.''

Marisa smiled wanly. "Thanks, Tracy, I can use the vote of confidence right about now.''

"And that Randall Block's a jerk, isn't he?'' Tracy inquired sympathetically.

Marisa laughed. "Well, he's a bureaucrat, forgive the pun. He goes back to Washington in the morning, thank God, and I hope he stays there.'' She sat up. "What do you say we hit that Italian restaurant on Evans Boulevard tonight? I could use a break from all this angst, and Charlie's picking up the tab.''

"You're on.'' Tracy rose and they headed for the door.

It was two more days before Marisa got in to see Jackson Bluewolf. His sister finally took pity on her— or got tired of seeing Marisa sitting in the visitors' lounge—and led her into Jack's room with a murmured, "I will probably regret this.''

Jack looked up as Ana said brightly, "Someone here to see you.'' She vanished immediately as Marisa stepped into the doorway.

Jack was propped against a pile of snowy pillows, his dusky skin a pleasant contrast with the stark white linens. The stands for intravenous fluids were still next to his bed but the tubes had been disconnected. He was stripped to the waist, his left shoulder swathed in bandages. Marisa was relieved to see that he was looking far from frail; in fact, he appeared rather remarkably hale and strong for a recent gunshot victim. And it was clear that he was angry. Very angry.

"What are you doing here?'' he demanded furiously.

"I... I." Now that she had finally made it into his presence, Marisa seemed to have nothing to say.

"I will have a few choice words to say to my sister for bringing you in here. Did you cast a spell on her?" he said.

"I just told her I wanted to see for myself that you were all right," Marisa replied.

"Well, you've seen me. I'm alive. You can go." He looked away from her pointedly.

"Is there anything I can do?" she said helplessly.

"Don't you think you've done enough already?" he countered.

"You know I never wanted this," Marisa said quietly, gesturing toward the bed.

"You wouldn't listen to me!" he snapped, stabbing a forefinger in her direction. "If you had, this never would have happened!"

"How nice for you that you know everything," Marisa said sarcastically, losing patience with his attitude.

"How nice of you to apologize!" he countered. "You can't even admit that you were wrong. God, I've heard of stubborn, but you are the living, breathing limit."

"Oh, come on, there was more to it than that and you know it!" Marisa replied with equal heat.

"What do you mean?" he said, his eyes narrowing. He pushed himself upright in the bed impatiently, the muscles in his upper arms flexing as he did so.

"I mean the flowers, the nifty rescue from the reporters, the practiced routine. Don't think I couldn't figure out the reason for all that attention."

He stared at her a long moment, his dark eyes penetrating, the hollows beneath them more pronounced from his recent illness. The shadow of stubble on his square jaw made him look even tougher than usual, and curiously even more attractive.

"Perhaps you'll enlighten me," he said quietly. Too quietly.

"You thought if you romanced me a little you could influence my conduct in the case," Marisa said bluntly.

There was a silence for several beats, and then he said flatly, "You must not have a very high opinion of yourself, Ms. Hancock."

"I don't know what you're talking about."

"Can't you think of any other reason for my 'attention,' as you put it, than my desire to best you in court?"

Marisa could feel herself flushing. She gripped her hands together, striving for equilibrium. "If you think I'm going to fall for that line, you're mistaken a second time," she replied unsteadily.

His mouth tightened. "Oh, the hell with you," he said disgustedly. "Get out."

"Wait a minute..."

He picked up the empty plastic carafe from his bedside table and threw it. The bottle exploded against the wall behind her head.

"I said get out!" he yelled.

Marisa stared at him, stunned. "You tried to hit me with that thing!" she gasped.

"If I were trying to hit you I would have hit you," he said through clenched teeth. "I merely want you to leave."

A nurse appeared in the doorway, staring in astonishment at the jug on the floor. "What the devil is going on in here?" she demanded.

"Remove this woman from my room," Jack said distantly. "She's making me sick."

The nurse looked at Marisa.

"I'm going," Marisa said meekly and slipped into the hall. The nurse followed her out.

"Miss, we can't have you upsetting the patients this way," the nurse hissed.

"Don't worry," Marisa said in defeat. "I won't be causing any further disturbances."

She hurried off down the hall before she could provoke any more flying missiles.


A couple of hours after Marisa's abrupt departure, Jack shoved his dinner tray aside and sat up on the edge of the hospital bed. The room swam for a moment and then righted itself. He glanced at the clock.

Twenty minutes before visiting hours began again, which meant that his mother and sister would be back. He sighed. He appreciated their good intentions, but after a while he usually couldn't think of anything to say to them.

He knew one visitor who wouldn't be returning. He closed his eyes resignedly. Had he actually thrown a bottle at her? He winced and shook his head. Soon he would be knocking her on the head and throwing her over his shoulder. Of course, that was what he really wanted to to; maybe the ancients had the best idea. They just acted, without worrying about the niceties of civilized behavior.

Marisa Hancock did not make him feel very civilized.

When she first left his room, he had been ready to give up on her entirely. But then he had replayed the preceding scene in his mind. He remembered the look on her face when he asked her if she couldn't think of the real reason for his attention. For one brief, glorious moment, she had known what he meant and wanted to believe him. And then her guard went back up and her expression changed to detached, cynical denial.

That one moment was enough to give him hope. When he was sprung from this cage he would find her and try again.

And he must make very sure to control his temper and not throw anything at her.

"So how did it go?" Tracy asked, looking up from her notes when Marisa entered their hotel room.

"Disaster, utter disaster. I should have listened to you and stayed away from him."

"Is he all right?"

"Oh, he's wonderful. He's in fine, even athletic, form," Marisa replied wryly.

"What does that mean?"

"Never mind. He's recovering nicely, that's what it means. I'm sure he'll be back tormenting us in court as soon as we resume the case."

"Which reminds me," Tracy said, brandishing an envelope with the seal of the State of Florida on it. "A little missive for you from Judge Lasky."

Marisa accepted it wearily. "Anything else?"

"Charlie called. He wants you to call him back at home tonight."

Marisa nodded.

"Oh, and the records from the Seminole cemetery have been released to the court. You can see them any time in Lasky's chambers."

"So he says here," Marisa observed, looking up from the letter. "Well, I guess we'd better get to it."

"Now?"

"Why not? Isn't that what we're here for?" Marisa said testily.

"Marisa," Tracy said gently, "the court is closed."

"In the morning, then. First thing."

Tracy nodded, certain that Marisa's mood had more to do with her visit to the hospital than her eagerness to peruse the history of an ancient graveyard.

Marisa spent the next day with the cemetery records and collapsed in her room that evening while Tracy went to the movies. She was staring at a rerun on television when there was a knock on her door.

"Just a minute," she called, pulling a dressing gown on over her pajamas and running her fingers through her tumbled hair.

There was no sound from the hall.

"Is that my laundry?" Marisa said, pulling the door open.

"I'm afraid not," Jackson Bluewolf replied.

Marisa stared at him, then glanced down in dismay at her bare feet and the washed-out robe she was wearing.

"I thought you were the cleaning service," she mumbled inanely.

By contrast with herself, he was gorgeous in eggshell jeans with a blue Oxford cloth shirt and leather moccasins. His left arm was in a sling and he carried a fringed suede jacket over his right shoulder.

"May I come in, anyway?" he asked.

# Three

"What are you doing out of the hospital?" Marisa asked, stepping aside so he could precede her into the room.

"I discharged myself against medical advice," he replied, turning to face her as she closed the door behind them. "I had to sign all these forms saying that my family would not sue them if I dropped dead in the street, or something like that."

"If I were your lawyer I would have talked you out of doing that," she said dryly.

He fished in his pocket and held up a bottle of pills. "I'm supposed to take two of these every four hours, or four of them every two hours. I forget." He frowned at the printing on the label.

"Please, sit down," Marisa said, sweeping a pile of papers from a chair onto the floor. "I don't want to witness a relapse."

He sat heavily as Marisa hovered nearby. They surveyed each other warily.

"Just give me a minute to change and I'll be right with you," Tracy said suddenly, remembering what she was wearing.

He nodded.

She bolted into the bathroom and grabbed a pair of jeans and a T-shirt from the hook on the back of the door. As she changed hastily, not bothering with underwear, she glanced at the mirror and groaned at her hair. She found a clip in the medicine cabinet and pulled it back, fastening the wavy mass at the nape of her neck. There was no time for makeup, she would have to do as she was. She reentered the bedroom as he looked up and said, "Too bad."

"What?"

"I liked you with your hair down."

Marisa fingered the clip nervously, resisting the impulse to yank it out and fling it on the floor.

"It was the first time I'd ever seen it that way. In court you're always so buttoned up and proper. With all that hair around your face you looked like a little girl."

Even if it was a deliberate attempt to charm her, she was helpless. It was working. Marisa looked back at him silently, unable to frame a reply.

"I suppose you're wondering what I'm doing here," he finally observed.

"The thought had occurred to me."

"I came to apologize for my behavior when you visited me at the hospital. I can only offer the excuse that I was shot full of prescription drugs and not responsible for my actions." He smiled slightly.

"That's all right. I got so mad at you I forgot to thank you for saving my life."

"That's a bit of an exaggeration."

"Not from my point of view."

"I guess we should call it even, then," he said lightly.

"Not even, exactly. That boy Jeff Rivertree is still in jail facing a capital charge."

He made a deprecating gesture. "That's my fault. When I guessed what Jeff was going to do, I rushed to the courthouse but I didn't arrive in time to prevent the incident. I had hoped to get to him first."

"What is he being held on?" Marisa asked.

"Attempted murder."

She winced.

"I hope we can get it reduced to felonious assault. We're trying to raise the bail right now," Jack said.

"I'd lobby for the lesser charge, but I can't get involved with his case. You do understand that," Marisa said.

He nodded. "I understand."

A silence fell and they stared at each other.

Jack cleared his throat. "There's another reason for my coming here," he said.

"Yes?" she said, sitting on the edge of the bed.

He leaned back in his chair and folded his good arm across the one in the sling. Instead of focusing on his face she found herself staring at the top button of his shirt, wishing she could undo it. When she tore her gaze away she realized that she didn't know what he was saying.

"Why this is so important to me," he concluded.

Marisa stared at him, clueless. "I beg your pardon?" she said weakly.

"Are you all right?" he asked.

"Yes, fine, I'm just a little tired. Hectic week, you know." She smiled vacuously, feeling a perfect fool.

"Of course. I was just saying that we've been at cross-purposes from the beginning, but I've never had a chance to explain to you why I'm involved here, why my work for NFN has become my life."

"Don't you do anything else?" Marisa asked ingenuously, and then bit her lip. "I'm sorry, I shouldn't have said that, but I know NFN can't be paying you much."

"Don't apologize, it's a perfectly logical question. As a matter of fact, you're right, my stipend from NFN is very small. I support myself with my writing."

"Writing?"

"Do you read mysteries?"

Marisa shook her head. "I'm afraid that my work doesn't leave much time for reading anything other than legal briefs."

"Well, I write a series of mysteries that features an Indian detective as the main character, sort of a Blackfoot Agatha Christie."

"You're Roger Whitemoon!" Marisa said incredulously. Even she had heard of him.

"Yes," Jack said, smiling. "I do a couple of books a year and that enables me to finance my NFN work, which occupies most of my time."

"The last one was a bestseller, wasn't it?" Marisa asked, impressed. "What was it called? *Quiet Prairie?*"

"*Silent Prairie*. Close."

"But your first love is the NFN."

He shrugged. "The books bring in the money, and I do enjoy writing them, but in the grand scheme of things the NFN is more important."

"Why?"

He sat forward, leaning his elbows on his knees. "I grew up on a reservation in Oklahoma. My father was killed when I was five and I was raised by my mother and older sister, whom you met."

Marisa nodded.

"You cannot imagine the hopelessness, the emptiness of the life there. Through a combination of circumstances I was able to escape it, but I never forgot it. I resolved to do what I could to change things for my people."

"But do you really think that the preservation of this cemetery is crucial enough to warrant spending eight million dollars to bypass it?" Marisa asked him.

His mouth tightened. "It's the principle involved, and anyway, the government can afford it."

"Eight million dollars?"

He stood up so swiftly that Marisa flinched. He began to pace the room and she watched him silently, noticing how the lamplight reflected off his seal black hair and threw his strong profile into relief against the wall.

"Do you think that any amount can make up for the abuses of the past?" he demanded. "There isn't enough money in the U.S. treasury to repay native Americans for what they've suffered, for being robbed of their homes and their land and being herded onto reservations like cattle. What do I care if it costs eight million or ten million or twenty million? They're not going to get one more yard of Indian land under any circumstances, and especially not this land, which has been sacred to the Seminoles for centuries." He ran out of breath suddenly and fell back into the chair, his face drained.

Marisa leaped to her feet. "I'm sorry, I shouldn't have brought this up tonight, you're obviously in no condition to discuss it."

"I'm fine," he said, irritated.

"Can I get you anything?"

He glanced around the room. "Do you have any coffee?"

"I'll order it from room service," she said.

"No, don't bother..." he began, but Marisa was already on the phone. When she hung up and turned back to him he was studying her intently, his dark eyes unfathomable.

"Coffee will be here in a few minutes," she announced.

"You must think me an awful bore," he said wearily, passing his hand over his eyes.

"Why do you say that?"

"I show up at your door, fresh out of the hospital, and even with one foot in the emergency room I can't stop berating you about my noble cause. Why haven't you thrown me out of here?"

"Jackson, you may be many things, but boring is not one of them," Marisa replied lightly.

"I like the sound of that," he said quietly, after a moment.

"What?"

"My first name on your lips. You've gone to great pains to avoid saying it."

"That was before you threw yourself in front of a bullet meant for me," she said.

"Don't be so dramatic," he said dryly. "Reality isn't quite as heroic. I was trying to shove you out of the way and I fell. That's the truth."

"The result is the same. You saved me." She leaned against the footboard of the bed. "How did you know what Jeff Rivertree was going to do?"

"His mother came to me and told me he had taken her husband's gun from the house. He had been sounding off about you in the bar the night his brother was killed and it didn't take much ingenuity to put two and two together."

"Sounding off about me?" Marisa asked.

"Yes."

"Saying what?"

Jack shifted uncomfortably.

"Tell me."

Jack met her eyes and then looked away.

"Hotshot gringa lawyer on the Washington payroll sent to overpower the impoverished Indians and deprive them of their inheritance?" Marisa suggested.

"Something like that," Jack confirmed.

"Isn't that what you think?" Marisa inquired evenly.

"Not any more," he replied, holding her gaze.

There was a knock at the door and the coffee arrived. Silence reigned as Marisa poured for both of them and Jack drained half his cup in one swallow.

"That's better," he said, sighing.

"You really should be home in bed," Marisa said worriedly.

"I've spent the last four days in bed," he said darkly.

"How is your shoulder?"

"Not bad. A little stiff."

Marisa watched him as he flexed the fingers of his injured arm and then looked up at her.

"So how did you get off the reservation?" she asked. "If you don't mind telling me, that is."

"I don't mind. It was the usual story. A teacher took an interest in me, helped me to get a scholarship."

"To college?"

"To a prep school first, then to college."

"I can't imagine you at a prep school," Marisa said, before she could censor herself.

"Cochise at Choate?" he said, raising one dark brow.

"I didn't meant that," she murmured, unable to meet his eyes.

"That was about the size of it. I didn't go to Choate, but the school was similar."

"Was it awful?" Marisa asked softly.

"I didn't exactly fit in with the preppies, but I endured it. I knew that it was my only chance and I took it."

"And college?"

He grinned. "Oh, college was different. I had a great time."

Marisa could imagine the swath he cut through the coeds. Her expression must have reflected what she was thinking because he said, "I became a significant minority experience for a number of female undergraduates, until I realized what was motivating them."

Marisa looked at him inquiringly.

"Curiosity," he said flatly. "Not very flattering certainly, but accurate. They weren't interested in me, but in something, or somebody, different."

"I'm sure that wasn't true of everyone," Marisa said quietly.

He tilted his head to one side. "How have you remained such an innocent, in your job?"

"In my job? I like that. I'm not exactly a hit woman for the mob, you know."

"But you've seen a side of life many women never encounter. Hasn't it changed you?"

Marisa thought about it. "I guess my experiences haven't exactly made it easy for me to trust people," she admitted.

He burst out laughing and the sound was so infectious that she had to smile, too.

"Tell me about it," he said, chuckling. "That first day when I tried to warn you there might be trouble you thought I was running you out of town."

"You wouldn't have been the first to try it," she said.

"So you're tough, eh?"

"Tough enough."

"You don't look tough. Right now you look like a tomboy about to play third base in a sandlot game."

Marisa's hand went to her hair self-consciously.

"Oh, leave it alone, I'm teasing you. You don't take much to teasing, either, do you?"

"I guess not."

"It's time someone loosened you up, took some of the steel out of your spine. Does that sober air come along with your sturdy New England roots?"

"You make me sound like some Puritan marching around in a mobcap and starched apron. Am I really so forbidding?"

"No," he said softly, his eyes lambent.

She had to look away.

"Have you always lived in Maine?" he asked in a normal tone, pouring himself more coffee.

"Yes, I was born there, in Freeport, and went to the University of Augusta. Now I work in Portland and live in Cumberland Foreside, a suburb a few miles out."

"Foreside?"

"Oceanfront."

"I see. So you're a real Yankee, the genuine article. With that accent and a name like Hancock, who could dispute it? Are you one of John's descendants?"

"The family claims so, but who knows? I have an aunt who's always doing genealogical charts. It's a cottage industry in the colonies. They draw them up for the tourists."

He smiled. "And where did Marisa come from?"

"My mother is French."

"An interesting combination." He put his cup aside and yawned. "I'm sorry," he said, rising. "The coffee did not have the desired effect, I feel . . ." He reached out suddenly and Marisa rushed to take his arm.

"Are you all right?" she asked anxiously.

"Little woozy," he mumbled. She led him to the bed and he sat on its edge.

"Is it time for some of your pills?" she asked.

He glanced blearily at his watch. "I guess so."

"You guess so?" she said, alarmed.

"Two, I think."

"Let me get you some water from the bathroom," she said, moving toward the door. She had trouble locating a clean glass and finally found a wrapped one in the medicine cabinet, then ran the water until it was cold. When she emerged with the drink in her hand she found him sprawled across her bed, fast asleep.

Marisa froze, staring at him, then crept closer, loath to disturb him. She felt guilty for keeping him talking to her when he was just out of the hospital, but the temptation to be with him, find out more about him, had been too great.

She set the glass on the lamp table and sat next to him on the bed, studying the sharp planes of his face, the hard line of his mouth now relaxed into sleep. He was not pretty, his individual features were bold and arresting rather than handsome, but somehow they worked in combination to make him the most attractive man she had ever met.

And now the most attractive man she had ever met was asleep on the bed in her hotel room.

What was she going to do?

She could try to wake him and take him back to wherever he was staying, but in his condition that would be a project, and his exhaustion was so apparent that she could not bear to wake him.

Making up her mind, Marisa drew the coverlet over his sleeping form and then hung the Do Not Disturb sign out for the staff. Remembering that Tracy would return later, she went through the connecting door to Tracy's room and left a note for her, asking her not to come through and saying that she would explain in the morning. Then she went back and checked on her charge.

Jack was sleeping peacefully, a slow pulse beating in his throat. Marisa found his jacket on the chair and rummaged in the pocket, locating his pills. They were a commonly prescribed painkiller, and since he seemed to be in no discomfort Marisa decided he could do without them. When she shoved the plastic vial back into his pocket a crumpled piece of paper fell out on the floor.

Feeling ashamed of her snooping, she nevertheless smoothed it out and read it.

"Rm. 232, ex. 1545" was scrawled on it in a boldly flowing, masculine hand.

It was her room number and telephone extension at the hotel. He had been carrying it around with him.

Marisa sat in the chair he had vacated, clutching the scrap as if it were a talisman.

This was all wrong, and she knew it. Jack was involved with her case and, furthermore, he was the opposition's staunchest supporter. So why didn't any of it seem to matter? Why was she willing to jeopardize case and career and future for a man she'd spent barely a few hours with, under the most unfavorable circumstances? It seemed to be the question of the hour, of her life, in fact.

Meanwhile, she had a guest.

Marisa took the clip out of her hair, switched off the lamp and locked the door of her room, and then slipped onto the bed next to Jack. She was sure she wouldn't sleep, but of course she did, too worn out from her emotions to stay awake. The last thing she remembered was the sound of Jack's breathing in the dark.

Jack woke first in the morning, grainy-eyed and disoriented, squinting at the unfamiliar curtains on the windows. He turned slightly, gasped at the pain in his shoulder, and then caught sight of Marisa, sleeping on her stomach beside him. It took him several seconds to sort out what had happened; then he sat up slowly to get a better look at Marisa, being careful not to shake the bed and disturb her.

Marisa's face was crushed into the pillow with one flushed cheek exposed, a tendril of fine blond hair trailing over it. She was fast asleep, lips parted to expose a row of teeth, one fist clutching the sheet like a child. Jack held back from touching her as long as he could, but the temptation was just too great. He slipped his hand under the weight of her hair and cupped the back of her neck.

Marisa stirred, then rolled over as he increased the pressure of his fingers. Her lashes fluttered and then lifted. She woke to find Jack leaning over her, his good arm beneath her shoulders.

His whiskey-colored eyes seemed to fill the world. The yearning in them so closely matched her own that no words were needed. She put her arms around his neck as he bent his head to kiss her.

His mouth was softer than she would have guessed, but his body was hard, lean and muscular, as he pressed her into the bed. She kept telling herself that she should pull away, but the delicious contact, so often imagined, was too wonderful to end. His shirt parted from his belt as he moved and her hand found the naked skin of his back, smooth and warm and supple. He groaned as she touched him and his lips traveled from her mouth to her neck; Marisa arched to expose more of her flesh to his caress. He pulled her tighter against him and she sighed luxuriously; not even the crackling of the bandage beneath his shirt gave her pause. She was too hungry and he was too expert, too eager. When he drew back and pulled her shirt up she was submissive until his hand slipped beneath it and found her bare breast. Then she gasped and stiffened, but he mastered her immediately, rocking her gently, his breath fanning her cheek.

"Please," he muttered. "Oh, please."

Marisa was undone. She was no match for him, especially when she wanted him so much. She lay back and lifted her arms; he was tugging her top off over her head when the telephone rang.

They both froze, like blowzy characters caught in the act in a French farce.

"Ignore it," Jack murmured, tightening his grip.

"It might be the office," Marisa said, coming to her senses, color flooding into her face as she glanced down at her disordered clothes. She struggled away from him and sat up, tucking her shirt into her jeans.

"Oh, damn the office," he muttered, falling back on the bed with his arm over his eyes.

Marisa grabbed the receiver. "Hello?" she said hoarsely.

"Marisa, is that you?" Charlie Wellman said.

She coughed, clearing her throat. "Yes."

"Are you coming down with a cold?" Charlie said.

"No, I'm fine. What is it, Charlie?"

"I sent you the files you requested by overnight mail, they should be there by noon. If they don't come to your room, check at the desk."

"Thanks, Charlie. I'm going over to the courthouse this morning and I should be able to give you the final figures on the cemetery removal plan in a couple of days."

There was a long pause at the other end of the line. "Marisa," Charlie said gently, "it's Saturday."

"Oh, right. Well, let's say by Wednesday, then."

"Is something wrong, kid?" Charlie said.

Marisa glanced at Jack, who was watching her through narrowed eyes, propped up on his good arm.

"No, of course not. Events have been moving so fast I'm just losing track of time."

"Are you sure you shouldn't come home? Every time I think about that boy taking a potshot at you I want to put you on the next plane. We'll find somebody else to take over down there."

"I want to finish what I started, Charlie."

"Okay. I can understand that. How is Bluewolf?"

"Out of the hospital," she said. And on my bed, she thought.

"Well, all right. I won't keep you. Give my best to Tracy."

"I will."

"Goodbye."

"'Bye."

"The long arm of Portland?" Jackson said dryly as she hung up the phone.

"Yes," Marisa said shortly.

"Oh, oh," Jack said, swinging his legs over the edge of the bed. "Is it my imagination or has the temperature in here dropped suddenly?"

"Please don't be glib, I don't think I could bear it," Marisa said, blinking rapidly. She was horrified to discover that she was on the verge of tears and turned away quickly so he wouldn't see.

Jack wasn't fooled. He took her by the shoulders and turned her around to face him.

"Hey, hey, what's all this?" he said, concerned.

"I'm . . . confused," she said, wiping at her eyes.

"I'm not," he said firmly. "I wanted you ten minutes ago and I want you now. What's the problem?"

She stared at him. "What's the problem?" she echoed. "Does the term 'conflict of interest' have any meaning for you?"

"That's an excuse," he said dismissively.

"I shouldn't even be talking to you outside the courtroom," she went on, "much less . . ." She trailed of unhappily.

"Much less what? Engaging in illicit sexual activities?"

"Oh, you really are vile," Marisa said disgustedly.

"I see. What happens now? Do the lady lawyer police show up and cuff me to the headboard?"

"I think you should go."

"Just like that."

"Yes, just like that. What else is there to say?"

"You might say you enjoyed our night together, and what followed this morning," he said calmly.

Marisa maintained a stony silence, not meeting his eyes.

"Marisa, what do you expect?" he demanded. "I'm not going to apologize for finally doing what I've wanted to do from the first moment I saw you."

"I'm not asking for an apology," she said.

"Then what? For me to act like last night never happened?"

She met his angry gaze squarely.

"Oh no. I'm not going to play 'let's pretend' with you," he said, shaking his head. "Let's pretend that Marisa is a legal robot, let's pretend that Marisa is an innocent little virgin without an active hormone in her body..."

Marisa slapped him, and then stared at her hand as if it had taken on a life of its own.

"Great," he said tightly, the imprint of her fingers still on his cheek. "Thanks a lot." He picked up his jacket and brushed past her, reaching for the door-knob.

"Wait." she said miserably.

"For what? Another smack?"

"Don't forget to take your pills, you missed the dosage last night," she said inanely.

"You're crazy, do you know that?" he said, his back still to her. "You wallop me for telling you the truth, and then you remind me to take my medicine?"

"I'm sorry I hit you," she whispered, her eyes swimming again.

He turned to face her, his jaw set. "Look, lady, I don't know why you can't admit it, but you want me. You want me as much as I want you, and the sooner you face that, the happier we both will be." He yanked open the door and bolted through it, slamming it behind him.

Marisa collapsed on the bed, wiping her eyes with her fingers. She could still see the imprint of Jack's head on the pillow next to hers.

It was several moments before she heard the insistent tapping coming from the next room.

"Marisa?" Tracy's voice said tinnily. "Are you all right?"

Marisa hid her face in the crook of her arm. Please God, she thought, no more. Then she got up and faced the inevitable.

Tracy was standing on the other side of the connecting door with her hands on her hips when Marisa opened it.

"Well?" Tracy said, waving the note Marisa left for her in the air. "What's going on?"

"Nothing."

"Nothing?" Tracy said, peering over Marisa's shoulder. "I heard voices, a man's voice and yours. Who was here?"

"Jack Bluewolf."

"What a surprise," Tracy said sarcastically, moving into Marisa's room. "Is he the reason I got this little missive?"

Marisa was silent.

"He spent the night here?" Tracy asked, her voice rising into a little squeak.

"It's not what you think."

"Oh, of course not. You played board games all night."

"He had just gotten out of the hospital and he was a little shaky. He fell asleep on my bed and I didn't want to move him, he needed the rest. That's all there is to it."

"Not all, from the expression on your face, sweetie. You look shell-shocked."

"We had sort of a fight before he left."

"I heard. And why did he come here to see you straight from the hospital?"

"Well, we had sort of a misunderstanding when I visited him there," Marisa explained awkwardly.

"I see. You had sort of a misunderstanding then sort of a fight this morning. You know what this means, don't you?"

"I'm losing my mind?" Marisa suggested feebly.

"Sexual frustration," Tracy said sagely.

"Oh, please." Marisa sat in the chair and contemplated her bare feet morosely.

"What, am I wrong? You're wildly attracted to him, aren't you? Why deny it?"

"I can't do anything about it, Tracy, you know the position I'm in! And he's so..."

"Aggressive?"

"Well, yes."

"Good for him," Tracy said firmly, and picked up the room service menu.

"Whose side are you on?"

"Yours, dearie. A man like this one is what you've needed for a long time."

"Counseling without a license again, Tracy?"

"What do you want for breakfast?" Tracy said, ignoring her.

"How can you think about food at a time like this?" Marisa demanded, outraged.

"A time like what?"

"I'm having a crisis here!"

"What's the crisis? You've finally met a man who can melt the icy reserve that's kept everybody else at a distance for as long as I've known you. More power to him. How about blueberry pancakes?"

"There's more, Tracy. He was trying to get me to admit how I felt this morning and I...well...I slapped him."

"You!" Tracy hooted. "Miss Cool, Calm and Collected? I would have paid good money to see that."

"I'm not going to get involved with him."

"You're already involved with him."

"I don't have to make it any worse. Aside from the ethical considerations, he's a lady-killer. I don't want to be used and then tossed away like a facial tissue."

"Uh-huh. What's the real problem?"

Marisa blinked. "What do you mean? I just told you."

"What did he say that made you hit him?"

"I don't remember."

"Yes you do."

"He said I was pretending to be an innocent little virgin."

Tracy burst out laughing.

"It's not funny."

"Don't you know that's the sort of thing men always say when they don't get their way? Forget it."

"I can't."

"Why not?"

"Because I'm not pretending, I am one."

"One what?" Tracy said, still reading the menu.

"Haven't you got that thing memorized by now?" Marisa snapped. "Are you listening to me? I'm not pretending, I am a virgin."

She had Tracy's full attention now. "You're joking," Tracy said, gaping at her.

"I'm not."

"You must be the only twenty-seven-year-old virgin in captivity," Tracy said, awed.

"Twenty-eight," Marisa said mournfully.

"I can't believe it."

"He'll laugh at me," Marisa said quietly.

"Oh, honey, no," Tracy said, putting the menu aside. "Don't think that way. It just makes you special, that's all."

"Specially odd."

"Haven't you ever been in love?"

"I was always so busy, with school and then work," Marisa said lamely.

"But some men must have tried."

"Oh, sure, but they never seemed . . . I don't know. Wonderful enough, somehow."

"But this one is."

"He must be. I can't stop thinking about him, and it's complicating this case no end."

"Well," Tracy said briskly, "you can't go on like this. You'd better deal with it, and fast."

"Charlie telephoned this morning and asked if I wanted to be recalled. He was worried about the shooting, and I could have taken the opportunity to extricate myself from this mess.''

''What did you say?''

''No.''

''Then you must want to stay.''

''I can't bear the thought of not seeing Jack again,'' Marisa whispered. ''But I'm so scared.''

''You know, Bluewolf is not opposing counsel and he's not the nominal plaintiff either. He's just an adviser. Technically, there's no reason you can't see him socially.''

''I'm not sure Charlie would view it that way,'' Marisa commented dryly.

''You're as familiar with the ethical rules as I am, you know I'm right. You're using all of that bar association mumbo jumbo as an excuse because you're afraid to deal with your feelings for this guy.''

''That's what Jack said. More or less.''

''He's right. You should call him.''

''Perish the thought.''

''What are you going to do, march back into court in ten days and act like none of this ever happened?''

''I have no choice.''

''Boy. I'm going to have a ringside seat for this one.''

''You, my dear, are going to be up to your ears in Florida reporters at the library.''

''Oh, come on, you have to let me audit in court sometime.''

''We'll see. And in the meantime, we're driving over to Crystal River today to depose the ex-custodian of the Seminole cemetery. He lives in a mobile-home park there with his granddaughter.''

''Busy, busy,'' Tracy said, picking up the menu again.

* * *

Marisa did not have to wait for the resumption of court proceedings to see Jack Bluewolf again. She and Tracy were having dinner in the hotel restaurant on Sunday night when he walked in with a statuesque redhead on his arm.

"Don't look now," Tracy confided over her chicken cordon bleu to Marisa, "but himself just arrived with Brenda Starr."

"What?" Marisa asked, taking a sip of water.

"I said, don't turn around but Jack is here."

Marisa stiffened but kept staring straight ahead. "Where?"

"Over your let shoulder, heading for a table in the corner. And he has a six-foot, auburn-haired Amazon with him."

"Tracy," Marisa said in exasperation.

"It's true. Well, five ten anyway, and she's wearing flats. Who the hell *is* that?"

"How should I know?" Marisa said testily.

"What a coincidence that he brought her here for dinner," Tracy said cynically.

"This hotel has one of the few decent restaurants in town," Marisa pointed out.

"Oh, and I suppose it has nothing to do with the fact that you're staying here. Seems like he decided to let you know you had some competition."

"How does he look?" Marisa asked.

"Has he ever looked bad?" Tracy countered. She speared a slice of ham and then dropped her fork on her plate. "I'm going to find out who this new arrival is," she said decisively, rising.

"Tracy!" Marisa hissed, but it was already too late. Tracy was halfway across the room. Marisa briefly debated the merits of a flying tackle and then subsided, contemplating murder instead. She pushed pieces of lemon sole around on her plate for an eternity until Tracy returned.

"I am going to flay you alive," she said flatly, as Tracy resumed her seat.

"Tut tut. Don't you want to know what I found out?" Tracy replied smugly, picking up her napkin.

"What did you do, get her to fill out a questionnaire?"

"Certainly not. I went over there and presented myself, expressing my regret about the Jeff Rivertree situation. Mr. Bluewolf, gentleman that he is, of course then had to introduce his companion."

"Well, who is she?"

"Aha. So you are curious."

"Tracy, you are about this close to getting my knife in your nose," Marisa said in a dangerously calm voice.

"All right, all right. She's a reporter from the *Miami Herald*. He's doubtless giving her a biased earful on the situation here."

"Doubtless."

"Anyway, they seemed real chummy. I think he knew her before this, maybe from some of his previous work or something. I wouldn't worry too much about her, I think she's had a nose job."

Marisa had to laugh. "How did you come to that conclusion?"

"A nose that perfect never existed in nature."

"What about Catherine Deneuve?"

"Well, there couldn't be two. And I'm sure she dyes her hair. Lovely Lady #32, Gentle Auburn. I detected roots."

"Did you take her blood pressure while you were at it?"

"And that dress is a knockoff, you can always tell."

Marisa stared at her balefully.

"What's this?" Tracy said brightly. They looked up to see the maître d' bearing down on them with a wine bottle deep in a bucket of ice and a towel draped over his arm.

"Compliments of the gentleman over there," he said courteously, and displayed the bottle.

Marisa couldn't look, but Tracy waved enthusiastically in the direction of Jack's table.

"Stop that," Marisa said in a low tone.

"Good stuff," Tracy said, examining the label.

"Please tell the gentleman, no, thank you, we don't drink," Marisa said primly.

"I drink," Tracy said.

Marisa kicked her under the table.

"But madame . . ." the maître d' said.

"Take it away," Marisa said firmly.

The man departed.

"You're no fun," Tracy said.

"I am not swilling down that man's liquor after he . . ." she trailed off into silence.

"You're just in a jealous snit because he showed up here with Miss Tallahassee," Tracy said. "Or Miami."

"I am not jealous."

"Uh oh," Tracy said.

"What now?" Marisa said despairingly.

"He's coming over here."

"Who?"

"Who do you think?"

Before Marisa could gather her wits Jack was at her elbow.

"Don't you like Chardonnay?" he inquired mildly. He was wearing a beige raw silk jacket with tailored slacks and an open shirt.

"I have no intention of drinking your wine," Marisa said flatly.

"Why not? It was just a friendly gesture."

"We're not friends."

"Some people might say that sending it back was the ungracious gesture of a spoiled brat," Jack said evenly.

"Some people might say that sending it over here in the first place was the flamboyant gesture of a self-satisfied prig," Marisa replied.

Tracy was transfixed, her head moving back and forth between Jack and Marisa as if she were observing a tennis match.

"Your assistant here could teach you some manners," Jack said.

Tracy sank a little lower in her chair.

"An ape could teach you some manners," Marisa observed crisply, shoving her chair back from the table.

"Where are you going?" Jack inquired.

"You're the mystery writer, you figure it out!" Marisa stalked past him and he followed her out into the lobby. From their respective tables, Tracy and Jack's erstwhile companion stared after the two of them in amazement.

Marisa charged into the ladies' room and Jack was right on her heels. A blue-haired matron gasped as Jack appeared in the mirror behind her. She dropped her lipstick into the sink.

"Relax, madam, I'm harmless," he said to the woman, holding up his hand.

"Don't you believe him!" Marisa snapped.

The old lady retrieved her lipstick and hurried to the door. "I'm calling security," she said huffily.

"You, madam, are perfectly secure," Jack said dryly.

The woman departed hastily after favoring Jack with a withering look.

"You're making a fool of yourself," Marisa said to him.

"Like you did yesterday morning?"

"I see that you recovered from that episode pretty fast," Marisa countered.

"What does that mean?" he demanded.

"Why did you choose to dine here this evening?"

"I suppose you think my coming here had something to do with you," he said.

"A suspicious woman might come to that conclusion."

"Don't flatter yourself."

"Drop dead." Marisa swept around him and through the door into the lobby once more. He shot out onto the tiled floor right behind her. Tracy was leaning against the wall outside the rest room and observed their passage with interest.

"Stop following me," Marisa said, rounding on Jack furiously. She caught sight of Tracy and added, "I'm going up to my room. Would you take care of the check?"

They both watched as Marisa rounded the corner for the elevator. A uniformed man wearing a badge labeled "hotel security" approached Jack and looked him over carefully, but since Jack was standing innocently in the hall, the security guard merely hesitated for a moment and then walked over to the desk.

"May I make a suggestion?" Tracy asked gently.

Jack turned to face her, thrusting his hands deep into his pockets. He shrugged wearily. "Please do."

"You're handling this all wrong."

He surveyed her archly. "No kidding."

"Marisa is not giving you the runaround."

He sighed. "You could have fooled me."

"Have you got a minute?"

Jack glanced toward the dining room where the red-head was waiting for him. "Sure. Come on, we'll go inside."

Tracy walked along with him and said, "You must have a very understanding date."

"She's not my date. She's my college roommate's wife."

"You didn't tell me that before," Tracy said, smiling.

He saw her glance and smiled slightly himself. "All right, I didn't tell you everything but I didn't lie. She does work for the *Miami Herald*. Just let me explain all this for a moment and then we can talk."

Tracy stood aside as Jack held a brief conversation with the woman, who grinned and rose, nodding at Tracy as she passed. When she had left, Jack pulled out a chair for Tracy and then sat down, facing her across the table.

"Okay, I'm all ears."

Tracy folded her hands on the snowy linen table-cloth. "Look, I think there's something we should get straight from the start. Are you seriously interested in Marisa, or are you just fooling around?"

"What are you, her mother?" Jack asked, amused.

"Answer the question."

He looked down for a moment, then up again, his expression now wary. "I'm serious," he said, as if he didn't want to admit it.

"And you think she's leading you on and then backing off at the last minute, playing teenage games with you."

He sat back in his chair and folded his arms. "I don't know if I would put it quite that way."

"Any way you put it, that's why you're annoyed, isn't it?"

He looked away, then nodded.

"All right. She would kill me if she knew I was telling you this, but she's not playing hard to get. She's scared."

"Of me?" Jack said alertly.

"Of a relationship with you. A physical relationship."

He stared at Tracy. "What are you saying? Was she...hurt? Raped?" He said the last word as if he were praying that it wasn't true.

"No. It would be her first time."

Jack's mouth opened. "Come on."

"It's true."

"I don't believe it."

Tracy turned her palms up slowly. "I was surprised, too."

"But she's a lawyer!"

Tracy made an exasperated gesture. "Do you think there's some sexual initiation that comes along with a bar association card?"

"No, but she's so competent and professional..."

"She's good at her job. Maybe too good, maybe that's why she's neglected other areas of development, in a manner of speaking."

"And she's so pretty," he murmured, as if to himself.

"That has nothing to do with it. The most promiscuous girl in my high school class was also the least attractive. What kind of thinking is that? How old are you, twelve?"

The sarcasm was lost on Jack, who was still sitting in the same position, as if stunned.

"Thinking about changing your tactics?" Tracy asked dryly.

He exhaled heavily. "I guess I'd better do just that."

"Wise choice," Tracy said, shoving back her chair. Jack rose in response. "Now don't let on that I told you this, or I warn you, I will be very close to death," Tracy added.

"Not a word."

Tracy made a fist. "Good luck."

Jack smiled charmingly, and Tracy wondered briefly why she was taking all this trouble to hand Jack to Marisa when she might have been going after him herself. Then she remembered. Friendship. That's what it was.

Tracy walked out of the dining room, pausing to pick up her check, as Jack sank back into his chair, his expression thoughtful.

When Marisa came downstairs the next morning on her way to Judge Lasky's chambers she found Jack sitting in the lobby sipping a cup of coffee. She tried to sail past him but he jumped up and blocked her path.

"Please let me go, I'm late," she said frostily.

"Five minutes," Jack said.

Marisa kept moving.

"Two minutes."

She wavered.

"One minute."

"Oh, all right." As she sat in the chair across from the one he had occupied she noticed the stack of folded newspapers and the paper napkin littered with crumbs.

"How long have you been sitting here?" she asked.

"A while."

Marisa looked at him.

"I thought if I came up to your room you would throw a fit, so I chose neutral ground."

She crossed her legs and folded her hands in her lap. "I'm waiting," she said.

Jack took a deep breath as Marisa concentrated on not staring at the breadth of his shoulders in the thin crewneck sweater or the muscular thighs revealed by his tight jeans. She wound up looking stupidly at the floor.

"Hey," he said gently, "I'm up here."

She raised her eyes to his face.

"That's better." He licked his lips, which made her look away again.

"Court doesn't resume until next week," he said, "and I wondered if in the meantime you would let me take you to dinner."

Marisa shook her head in wonderment.

"Don't look like that, I promise to behave," he said.

"You know it's a bad idea."

"Why?"

"Well, how have we been getting along so far?" she asked rhetorically.

"We got along great when I slept overnight in your room," he said softly.

"That was simply an accident. I won't put myself in that situation again."

"Look, I'm talking about dinner, that's all. You have my word that I will not barge into any rest rooms and will refrain in general from making a nuisance of myself."

She smiled thinly.

"That's better. What do you say?"

Marisa hesitated. She had vowed never to fall for his blandishments again, but how could she resist him as he sat there wearing the half smile that melted her so effectively? He was winning, and he knew it.

"All right," she said.

He stood triumphantly. "Eight o'clock tomorrow night. A friend of mine has a boat I can borrow, we can take a sunset cruise up the inland waterway to a restaurant I know on the water. Can you swim?"

"Yes. Will I have to?"

He grinned. "Let's hope not, but it's best to make sure first."

"Is it a fancy place?"

He shrugged.

Marisa gazed at him in exasperation. She had never known a man who could answer that question. "Is a jacket required for men?"

He nodded.

"Okay, that tells me what I need to know."

"I'll meet you here in the lobby at eight. All right?"

"Fine."

He smiled at her one last time and then strode purposefully across the hotel's Oriental carpet, a man who had achieved his goal.

"If a jacket is required for men it's a pretty fancy place," Tracy said, shoving hangers to the right and left along the rack. "Get something with a little zip." She selected an azure blue cocktail dress with rhinestone straps and held it up for Marisa to see.

"That's entirely too much zip for me," Marisa said.

They were in the hotel boutique looking for an outfit for Marisa's date with Jack. She had brought along only professional clothes and had nothing to wear. Or at least that's what Tracy was insisting.

"I could always wear my gray silk suit," Marisa suggested. "With a fancier blouse it would be all right."

"You don't want to look 'all right,' you want to look smashing. Besides, gray is for nuns. How about this?" She held up a coral chemise with a side slit and a deep vee neck.

"No, thanks." Marisa pulled out a navy featherweight wool with a white satin bib and satin cuffs. "Look, this has satin on it, is that fancy enough for you?"

"Are you giving the eighth-grade commencement speech?" Tracy asked, surveying the garment with distaste.

"I'm trying it on," Marisa said stubbornly.

"Fine. Take this too." Tracy handed her a pale blue silk dress with a fitted waist and a tulip hem. The only decoration was a dusting of seed pearls on the shoulders. It was simple but elegant.

"That's pretty," Marisa conceded.

"Thank God," Tracy said fervently.

Marisa disappeared into the dressing room. When she emerged in the navy dress Tracy groaned.

"I like it," Marisa said.

"You would."

"It's very practical, I could wear it to court."

"Exactly my point. What you do not want for this occasion is a dress you could wear to court."

"It's on sale."

"Honey, you look like Hester Prynne in that dress. All you need is the red brooch. Put it back."

Marisa returned to the dressing room and came out again in the blue silk.

"Now you're talking," Tracy said approvingly.

Marisa turned and looked at herself in the three-way mirror. The material clung to her in all the right places, the color lit her eyes and flattered her complexion, and the skirt described a graceful arc above her knees.

"Pilgrim, your search has ended," Tracy said.

"It's too short," Marisa said feebly.

"Buy it," Tracy said firmly.

Marisa glanced at the price tag and gasped.

Tracy opened her purse, took out her wallet, and extracted a credit card.

"If you don't buy it, I will," she said.

"Don't bully me, I'll make up my own mind," Marisa said, annoyed. She marched into the dressing room and came out a few minutes later attired in her own clothes. She brought the two dresses over to the clerk and said, "I'll take the silk."

Tracy chuckled.

"I needed something dressier anyway," Marisa said defensively.

"Of course. Who doesn't?"

"I'm not sure which shoes will go with it."

"We'll find something."

"I don't have the right jewelry."

"My pearl earrings will be perfect," Tracy said. She giggled and rolled her eyes. "He is going to die when he sees you in that. I'd love to be there."

Marisa said nothing, wishing that she were as confident as Tracy that the outfit would be a success.

Marisa's doubts were erased when she saw Jack's expression as he met her in the lobby. She had resisted the temptation to put her hair up and instead let it fall loosely over her shoulders, and she wore her highest heels. Jack's eyes passed over her from head to foot and then back up to her face.

"You look incredibly lovely," he said softly.

He was wearing a navy jacket with a white shirt, tan slacks and a rep tie. The combination with his vivid features was memorable. Cochise at Choate. Marisa had to restrain herself from running into his arms.

"Shall we dance?" he said, extending his hand.

She took it and they walked out into the balmy night.

# Four

"The boat is docked right across the street," Jack said, indicating the public pier, which was within view of the hotel.

"Should I have brought another pair of shoes?" Marisa asked, glancing down at her highly unsuitable pumps.

"No, it's high tide. You can just step into the boat. When the tide is out you have to climb down a ladder."

"Quite a trick in this outfit," Marisa said.

"That's why I suggested this time of day," Jack said.

"You mean you had already checked the tide charts?" Marisa asked, as they walked down the wooden dock.

"Yes." He took her hand and helped her step over a coiled rope someone had left in their path.

"You were confident."

He stopped and looked at her, his form backlit by the blazing sunset. "Hopeful," he corrected.

Marisa let it go at that. She stood looking across the water, her hair lifted by the light evening breeze, the sound of gulls and other seabirds filling her ears. She inhaled deeply of the salt air.

"What is it?" Jack asked.

"Everything is so beautiful," she said softly.

"Yes, everything is," he agreed, gazing at her.

"I love the sea," she said.

"Maine natives usually feel that way."

She smiled and nodded.

"Did you have boats while you were growing up?" Jack asked.

"Sailboats. My grandfather thought powerboats were an abomination."

Jack jumped down into the boat and then held out his hand to Marisa. "He would never have approved of this one."

Marisa stepped into the boat and watched as Jack undid the spring line and then flipped on the blower switch. He lifted the cover on the engine to check it for leaks and then switched on the motor. The boat rumbled into life.

"Are you sure you know how to operate this thing?" Marisa asked nervously, feeling the vibrations beneath her feet.

"Do you doubt it?"

"Oklahoma has never been famous for its coastline," she pointed out uneasily.

Jack grinned. "I have a local friend who has taken me out in this several times," he said.

"How many times is several?"

"Will you relax? For a Maine lady you're very twitchy." He undid the bowlines and fixed them to the posts in the slip and then freed the stern lines and tossed them onto the dock.

"Here we go," he said, stepping behind the wheel and guiding the boat out of the slip.

"What kind of boat is this?" Marisa asked, watching as they passed the fuel dock and headed out into the river.

"Twenty-foot Sea Ray Bowrider, dual two-fifty Mercruiser engine," he replied.

"That was a big help."

He chuckled. "You asked."

Once on the open water, the breeze picked up and Marisa became fascinated with the river traffic passing around them. Jack cruised slowly until they had passed the No Wake area and then gunned the motor, accelerating until Marisa's hair was flying behind her like a flag. He looked over at her and she grinned delightedly.

"Like it?" he called.

"Love it," she replied.

There was little conversation for most of the trip since it was difficult to be heard over the roar of the motor and the wind. After about ten minutes Jack slowed the boat and turned into a narrow passage hemmed in on either side by marsh grass and weeds.

"What's this?" Marisa asked.

"The inland waterway. It was dredged by the Army Corps of Engineers, but even at high tide there are some shallow areas. It can be tricky in here."

"Tricky?" Marisa said warily.

"Relax, counselor. Open up that compartment and hand me the chart inside, will you? It looks like a map with lots of numbers on it."

"I know what a chart looks like," she said stoutly.

"Forgive me." He extended his left hand and Marisa gave him the chart. He unfolded it, frowning slightly, and then stabbed at it with his finger.

"See here? Four feet deep. This boat draws three feet, so even if the chart is just a little bit off, or if the bed has shifted, we could get into trouble."

"Trouble?" Marisa said weakly.

"We could go aground," he said, guiding the boat slowly forward. Greenery pressed in on either side and birds splashed in the tide pools on the shore. There was an eerie silence, punctuated by the chirping of crickets and the distant racketing of cicadas.

"Then why did you come this way?"

"It's shorter, for one thing, and I want to make our reservation. It's a prettier trip, too."

"What happens if we go aground?"

"Same thing that happens in a sailboat. Got to get her off the bar and into deeper water."

"Wouldn't it have been a lot easier just to drive?" Marisa said logically.

He laughed. "Would you stop being such a lawyer for once? Where's your sense of adventure?"

"I think I left it back at the hotel."

"You just said you loved this trip."

"That's when we were going thirty miles an hour in open water," she replied.

There was a grinding sound and Jack said, "Damn."

"What?"

"I think we're stuck." There was a whirring noise as he raised the engine and then gunned the motor slightly. Nothing happened. He shut the engine off resignedly.

"Yup," he said, and yanked on his tie. Marisa watched as he undid the knot and pulled it off and then began to unbutton his shirt.

"What are you doing?" she asked, aghast.

"Got to go in and push her off," he said. She watched as he stripped off the rest of his clothes in the fading light, tossing them onto the pilot's seat. She looked away when he got to his pants, glancing back quickly to see him standing barefoot in a pair of black briefs, looking down at the water. Then he flipped a switch on the instrument panel and vaulted over the side in one swift motion. She heard the scattered splash as he hit the surface.

Seconds later the boat began to rock, and then she heard a loud thud. This was followed by an eerie silence. Marisa waited, ticking off the seconds, which lengthened into minutes. She was just about to jump in after him when Jack appeared in an explosion of spray. He swam strongly a few feet and then grabbed the steel ladder at the rear of the boat. He ascended it swiftly and clambered over the back to land beside her, dripping.

Marisa flung her arms around his neck.

"Hey, hey, what's all this?" he said softly, holding her off to look down into her face. "You'll ruin that pretty dress."

"Forget the dress, I thought you were drowned." She hugged him closer, pressing her face into his damp shoulder.

"Drowned! I was gone two minutes!"

"But I heard this thud, and then you didn't come back . . ." She trailed off miserably into silence.

"All right, all right," he said soothingly, rubbing her back with the flat of one large hand. "I was just swimming under the boat to find where it was caught. I switched on the bottom lights so I could see."

"So are we free?" she inquired finally, lifting her head and looking around warily.

"We are. Can't you feel the boat drifting?"

"You must be cold," Marisa said, stepping back, suddenly conscious of the way she was clinging to him.

"Not while you were holding me," he said quietly.

"Are there any towels?" Marisa asked briskly, eager to change the subject now that her fear had passed.

"In the duffel bag, over there," he replied, going to the wheel and starting the engine, steering the boat to the center of the passage. Marisa found a thick beach towel and came up behind him to drape it around his neck.

"Thanks." He looked over his shoulder. "What do you think, am I a dull date?" he asked, grinning.

"Never."

"For my next trick..." he said threateningly.

"Please, spare me."

He guided them through the rest of the narrow passage and then back into open water. He switched on the bow and stern lights as full dark fell around them.

"So much for my clever plan to take the scenic route," he said, shrugging. "We'll go back the other way, the passage is deeper."

"Okay."

"Sorry about scaring you."

"I'm over it now. Actually, it was kind of... interesting."

"Now that it's over?"

"Now that it's over," she agreed.

Marisa came up behind him and tucked the towel more closely around him. "Is that better?" she asked.

"Much," he replied quietly. He turned and faced her. "I guess I should get dressed. They probably won't let me into the restaurant this way." He shut off the engine and let the boat drift as Marisa handed him his shirt. He looked down at her as he shrugged into it.

"You were really worried back there?" he asked.

"Yes."

They were inches apart, seemingly the only two people abroad on the dark water, even though other boats were passing in the background all the time.

"I didn't bring you there to ravish you among the reeds," he said softly.

"If you wanted to ravish me, you already had a golden opportunity," she replied.

"But I do," he said, pulling her into his embrace again. Marisa wrapped her arms around his torso under the open shirt and laid her cheek against his chest.

"I do want you terribly, and that's been the source of all our conflicts, you know that," he said.

"I know," she murmured.

"Because you want me, too."

She nodded silently.

"What are we going to do about it?" he asked huskily.

"Go on to dinner?" she said desperately, drawing back reluctantly to look up at him.

He pushed a lock of her wind-disordered hair off her forehead. "All right," he said, and bent swiftly to kiss her cheek. "Let's get this tug into harbor." He dressed quickly, draping his tie around his neck, and then started the engine again. A short time later he turned into a canal and pulled up to the dock of a brightly lit restaurant. Tiny Christmas lights were strung along the waterfront and Leduc's was spelled out in neon along the Acadian roof of the building.

Jack tied up the boat and then shrugged into his jacket, glancing at Marisa.

"Feels like something's missing," he said.

"Your tie," she said, gesturing.

"Got a mirror?" he asked, feeling for it around his neck.

Marisa took a compact out of her purse and held it for him as he tied his tie.

"I'm helpless without a mirror," he said, grimacing. "In school I met guys who could do this blindfolded, but the technique has always eluded me."

"Can you see?"

"Are you kidding?" he said, tightening the knot. "You could do brain surgery on this dock." He looked up and squared his shoulders. "Okay?" he said.

Much better than okay, she thought. "Fine," she said. Marisa glanced into the mirror to make sure her makeup hadn't been smeared by Jack's wet shoulder, then replaced the compact in her purse.

Jack helped her out of the boat and they walked hand in hand to the door, which was flanked by evergreens bearing more Christmas lights. There was a giant wreath on the door.

"I had almost forgotten about Christmas. It's easy to do in this weather," Marisa said. "What date is it?"

"December twenty-fifth."

She shot him an exasperated glance.

"Three weeks away, Ebenezer," he added.

"That explains the large decorated tree in the lobby of the hotel," she said dryly.

"Don't you spend Christmas with your family?" he asked. "I had pictured a greeting card scene, traditional New England holiday, snow falling and chestnuts roasting on the open fire, kiddies gathered 'round the hearth..."

"Actually, there isn't any family, not anymore. My grandfather raised me after my parents died and he passed away three years ago. He left his house to me."

"So what do you do on holidays?"

"Oh, I have friends," she said vaguely.

Once they were inside, the captain seated them immediately at a table overlooking the water. The tablecloths were pink linen, the glasses were crystal, and the silverware was heavy and plentiful.

"Have you been here before?" Marisa asked.

"A couple of times with Ben Brady."

"This looks like Ben's type of place. Did you dissect me along with the *salade Niçoise?*" Marisa said archly.

Jack favored her with a secretive smile. "Actually Ben admires your ability very much."

"I'm sure that's not what he said."

"He said that your legs give you an unfair advantage with male jurors," Jack replied, grinning wickedly.

Marisa rolled her eyes. "That sounds like Ben."

"Oh, Ben's all right. He just resents his male preserve being invaded, especially by a woman who's as good at his job as he is."

"Better."

Jack laughed.

Marisa stared down at her menu, frowning. "What do you recommend?" she asked.

"*Coq au vin, coquilles Saint Jacques, trout alman-dine, flounder Provençale...*" he recited.

"No chicken nuggets?" she asked.

"Afraid not."

"That's all I usually have time for when I'm work-ing."

"You're not working now," Jack said, holding her gaze across the table.

She nodded. "I'll have the trout, with a salad."

When the waiter arrived, Jack gave their order and the waiter asked if they wanted to see the wine list.

"Still not drinking?" he asked Marisa, with a side-long glance.

"Don't start."

"Never mind," Jack said to the captain. "Bring the lady a club soda with lime and me a beer."

"Do they have beer in this place?" Marisa whis-pered after the man was gone.

"Imported beer."

"Of course."

"French beer."

"*Ça va.*"

"*Deux Magots,* by name."

"*D'accord.*"

They were both laughing when the waiter brought a "relish tray." It was a highly polished silver salver with a pile of thin, almost transparent biscuits on one end. There were several depressions lined with cut glass dishes containing various unidentified substances on the other.

"Mademoiselle?" the waiter said, offering it.

Marisa pointed.

"Pâté," the waiter said.

Marisa looked at Jack. He shrugged. "Goose liver."

Marisa pointed again.

"Escargot," the waiter said.

"Snails," Marisa said.

"Snails," Jack agreed.

"And is this caviar?" Marisa asked, indicating another dish.

"Beluga," the waiter said proudly.

Marisa waved the tray away.

"That assortment was relish?" she said, when the waiter was gone. "You wouldn't put it on hot dogs."

"I thought you said your mother was French," Jack said, chuckling, as he helped himself to a bread stick.

"French from Canada, the come-down-from-Quebec-to-work-in-the-woollen-mill type of French," Marisa said. "Not this kind."

"I see."

"You hang out in places like this?" she asked.

He shook his head. "Not really. I've been to them in New York, with book people sometimes, but not often. I was trying to make you feel comfortable."

They stared at each other.

"Want to head out of here and grab a burger someplace?" he said, smiling.

"Good idea."

He signaled the waiter, told the astonished man that they were going, and left a ten dollar bill for their drinks. When they were back outside in the neon moonlight, they looked at each other and chuckled conspiratorially.

"There's a sandwich place down the street with sawdust on the floor," Jack said.

"That sounds about right."

"Do you want to walk?"

"Sure. But can the boat stay where it is?"

"It's a shared marina, the dock serves all these businesses. Unless the maître d' runs out and sinks it for spite, it will be okay."

"We're a tad overdressed for sandwiches."

"Let 'em stare." Jack offered his hand and Marisa took it. They walked out into the street.

"You've managed to get around since you've been in Florida," Marisa commented.

"I always get around," he replied.

"I guess your work takes you everywhere."

"Pretty much."

"Do you like that, traveling all the time?"

He looked over at her. "It has its advantages."

"Meeting lots of people?"

"Meeting people like you."

"Women, you mean?"

His gaze narrowed. "Is this a trap, counselor?"

"I just wanted to know, that's all."

"Why?"

"Something tells me that the experience you're having with me is not uncommon for you."

He stopped walking. "The experience I'm having with you?" he said coolly.

"Well, you know . . ." Marisa began, backpedaling.

"I haven't had this 'experience' before, Marisa," he said flatly.

"I put it badly."

"I would say so."

"I'm not very good at this," she admitted.

"What?"

"Talking to men."

"Tell that to Ben Brady. He still bears the scars."

"You know what I mean. Talking to men in a social situation."

"You're all business, eh?" he said.

"Usually."

"Well, Ms. Hancock, that is about to change." They arrived at the luncheonette and he put his arm above her head to push the door open for them.

The room was filled with locals, who turned and stared at them blankly. Everyone was dressed casually and a haze of cigarette smoke hung in the air, which was heavily permeated with the yeasty smell of beer. Dead silence prevailed as they became the focus of all eyes. Marisa felt as if she were wearing a bridal gown at a funeral.

"So, I guess everybody knows we're here," Jack said in a low tone in Marisa's ear.

"That's my guess, too."

A waitress approached, removing a pencil from behind her ear and examining them with interest.

"Y'all comin' from a party?" she asked.

"You might say that," Jack replied.

"Dint they feed you theyah?"

"Not much."

"Then ya come to the raght place. Fallah me." They trailed in her wake to a back table which looked out over the water. A dilapidated dock sported a raft of fishing poles propped in place and a much abused rubber dinghy bobbing at anchor.

"Wonderful ambience," Jack said to Marisa.

"Whut's thayat?" the waitress inquired.

"Good food here," Jack said.

"Ya got that raght," she said. "Somethin' ta drink?"

"Iced tea," Marisa replied.

"Make that two," Jack said.

"Gotcha," the waitress said and ambled away.

"Menus?" Jack called after her.

"On the board," she sang and jerked her thumb in the direction of a chalkboard to their left.

"The caviar starting to look a little better?" Jack said to Marisa, grinning.

"What's a 'toad in the hole'?" Marisa asked, craning her neck to read.

"God knows. What's 'redeye gravy'? I'm afraid to ask."

"I like your idea. Let's get hamburgers. Everybody knows what a hamburger is."

"I wouldn't count on it."

The waitress returned with their tea.

"Well?" she said, her hands on her hips, surveying Jack with undisguised lust.

"Two burgers please, rare for me and..." he looked at Marisa.

"Medium well," Marisa said.

"Pickle?" the waitress said.

"I beg your pardon?"

"Ya'll want a pickle with thayat?"

"No, thank you," Marisa said.

"Slaw relish?" the waitress said.

"No."

"Grits?" she went on, shifting her feet.

Marisa looked at Jack, who was trying hard not to laugh.

"Chips?" the waitress said. "No estra chahge."

"Just the burgers," Jack said in a strangled voice.

"Gotcha." She drifted off, humming.

Jack collapsed in soundless laughter.

"Is this what the tourist guides mean by local color?" Marisa asked, giggling.

"I think this is it. Should we go?"

"Let's stick it out," Marisa said. "If I walk out of two places in one night it will make me think I'm difficult to please."

"We could always go back to the hotel, if you want."

"Oh, no," Marisa said, looking past him.

"What?"

"She sings, too."

Jack followed the direction of Marisa's gaze. Their waitress was ascending a small platform at the front of the room with a guitar around her neck.

"I hope she put our order in first," Jack said.

The waitress launched into a rendition of "The Midnight Special" that was evidently a favorite with the audience. She was actually quite a good singer, and when the food came, it was even better. The waitress's set was followed by a three-piece band playing ballads.

"Do you want to dance?" Jack said.

Marisa abandoned her half-eaten hamburger and joined him on the dance floor. When she stepped into his arms it felt as if she were coming home. He smelled of soap and starch and salt water from his dip. As the music went on they drew closer and moved less, until they were almost standing still in a fixed embrace.

They went through "Unchained Melody" and "Mona Lisa" and "Moon River," Marisa's head resting on Jack's shoulder, before the waitress marched up to them and tapped Jack imperiously.

"Will y'all be wantin' anythin' else?" she said.

"No, thank you," Jack said, as Marisa stood silently within the circle of his arms.

The waitress ripped a sheet off her pink check pad and handed it to him, then stalked away.

"Was that a hint, do you think?" Jack asked Marisa, grinning down at her.

"I think she wants us to pay up and leave," Marisa said.

He glanced at his watch. "It's eleven o'clock."

"They must be closing."

The band launched into "Good Night Ladies."

"That's definitely a hint," Jack said dryly.

Jack paid the check and they wandered out into the crystalline, chilly air.

"What a glorious night," Marisa said.

"Are you cold?" Jack asked.

"A little."

"Want my jacket?"

Marisa hesitated.

"Grits? Slaw relish? Chips?" he said.

"I'll take the jacket," Marisa answered, shaking her head at his nonsense.

He slipped it around her shoulders and she snuggled into its silk-lined warmth. Jack pulled his tie loose and unbuttoned the top button of his collar.

"Look at those stars," he said, as they walked down the deserted street back to the dock.

"I've never seen so many."

"At home, when you camp out on the prairie, you see more stars than you ever could in the city because there's no competition from artificial light. It makes me wonder what my ancestors saw when they roamed the plains before . . ."

"We came and ruined everything?" Marisa suggested.

He picked up a stone and tossed it away aimlessly. "I don't blame you for it personally."

"You shouldn't. My relatives always lived in Maine."

"Then they were killing off the Penobscots instead of the Blackfeet. Only the location changes."

"Does that bitterness keep you going?" Marisa asked softly, studying his grim expression.

"If I don't let it show too often." He shrugged. "Nobody likes a whiner."

"Justifiable rage is not whining."

"Yeah, but rage has to be controlled to be productive," he said. "Sometimes the control slips."

"I don't blame you."

"I blame myself." He stopped when they reached the dock and gazed out across the water. "I don't want to be a cliché. You know, wild Indian. It's what they expect, and I won't be what they expect."

"Traveling all the time, no fixed home, moving from case to case and cause to cause. It must make for a hard life," Marisa said.

" 'We cannot expect to be translated from despotism to liberty in a feather bed,' " he said, quoting.

"Thomas Jefferson," Marisa said.

He looked at her sharply. "Yes."

"My idol," Marisa said. "I was devastated in junior high when I found out he kept slaves."

"He was a Southern planter in the late-eighteenth century," Jack said cynically. "Who did you think was doing all the work while Thomas wrote those fine letters you were reading?"

"I guess I was naive."

He snorted.

"You were just quoting him," Marisa pointed out defensively, folding her arms.

"There were flaws in his life-style, common to all those of his class and culture. I can still appreciate the brilliance of his mind."

"The control you just mentioned before, will it slip if you lose this case?"

He turned and looked at her, his face set. "We won't lose," he said flatly.

Marisa felt a chill that had nothing to do with the night air. "Let's not talk about it," she said quietly. "I promised myself that we wouldn't talk about the case tonight."

"Good idea." He jumped down into the boat and readied it for the trip, then held up his hand to her. She stepped onto the runner and when she paused he bent and slipped his arm under her knees.

"Hold on," he said, as he lifted her into the well. In a second she was deposited on the seat and he was moving toward the wheel. She pulled his jacket closer around her as he undid the lines, and then they were moving swiftly through the water.

Jack's mood seemed to have changed, perhaps because reality had intruded with their discussion of the case. He concentrated on piloting the boat and they were back at the marina too soon.

"Are you just going to leave it there?" Marisa asked, looking back over her shoulder as they walked away from the boat.

"That's where it belongs. It's the regular slip where my friend keeps it," he said.

"Who's your friend?"

"The husband of the redhead you saw with me in the hotel dining room," he replied.

"She was a decoy, wasn't she?"

"Decoy?"

"You were trying to make me think she was your date."

"Did it work?"

"No."

He burst out laughing. "Liar."

"Well, maybe it worked a little," she admitted, and he put his arm around her shoulders, hugging her.

The traffic in the area of the hotel had died down considerably because of the late hour. They walked through the deserted lobby and took the elevator up to Marisa's floor alone. Their feet made no noise on the plush carpet as they walked to her room.

"I had a lovely time," Marisa said, giving him her hand as he turned to face her.

"If a bit unusual?" he said.

"That's part of what made it lovely."

He took her hand and placed her palm against his cheek. He closed his eyes.

"I don't want to leave you here," he said.

Marisa said nothing. At that moment she would have gone anywhere with him.

"When you come out in the morning you should find an arrow by your door," he said, smiling slightly.

"What?"

"Old Blackfoot custom," he replied. "When a brave picked out a special maiden, he would leave an arrow with his identifying feathers by her hogan as a proposal. When she found it, if she then ignored it, his proposal was considered rejected. But if she took it back to him they got married."

"I wouldn't reject you," Marisa said softly.

"I don't suppose I can come in," he said.

"You know what would happen."

"I want it to happen."

"Jack..."

"I know, I promised to behave. Can I see you tomorrow?"

"I have to work tomorrow."

"Court's not in session."

"I have to prepare, Jack. That's why I'm here. A court case is ninety percent preparation, and it's my responsibility to do it."

"Let Tracy take over."

"I can't."

"All right, all right. Tomorrow night, then."

"Where do you want to go?" she asked.

"Anywhere."

"What do you want to do?"

"Anything."

She sagged against the door, defeated. "Okay. I've been wanting to see that gallery that shows Seminole art...."

"Fine, we'll go there. What time can I call for you?"

"Seven."

"Fine."

"Jack, let's not drag this out. You'd better go."

"Am I permitted to kiss you good night?"

She was reaching up for him as his lips met hers. He tried to kiss her lightly, but it was no good; they were both too hungry. In just seconds Marisa was backed against the wall and he was pressing into her, his body hard and urgent as she clung to him.

Then he stepped back abruptly. "I can't do this," he said. "I'm too old to make love in hallways. Either let me come in or send me away."

"Jack..."

"All right. I'll see you tomorrow evening. Good night." He turned and almost ran off down the corridor, as if afraid that he would turn back to her.

Marisa sagged against the wall dreamily, then unlocked the door of her room. She walked through it in a daze, then stopped short.

Tracy was sitting cross-legged on her bed, wearing an oversize football jersey and eating a muffin.

"So?" she said, looking up. "How did it go? Tell Mother."

# Five

—

"Tracy," Marisa said wearily, "why aren't you in bed?"

"I am in bed," Tracy replied through a mouthful of crumbs, gesturing at her surroundings.

"You're in *my* bed," Marisa said, dropping her purse on a table.

"Details. Was the dress a hit?"

"It was."

"I knew it! He must have thought he was hallucinating after seeing you in those Mother Hubbards you wear to court."

"He was very complimentary."

"Where did you go?"

"Leduc's."

"Wow! That's a fancy place."

"How do you know?"

"Unlike you, I watch television. That place is always advertising on the local station. What did you have? Pheasant under glass?"

"A hamburger."

Tracy stared at her.

Marisa collapsed into a chair and stretched her legs out in front of her, kicking off her shoes.

"Neither one of us was really comfortable there, so we wound up in a juke joint down the street," she said.

"And?"

"And we danced, and we talked, and oh, on the way there the boat ran aground..."

"Sounds like a dream date," Tracy said sarcastically.

"Actually, it was. I didn't want him to go home. I wanted to bring him right in here...."

"Where you would have found yours truly," Tracy said pointedly.

Marisa shrugged and nodded. "We're going out again tomorrow night," she said.

"Good!"

"I had to think of something to do, so I said we'd go to an art gallery downtown."

"Uh-huh," Tracy said, sipping milk from a glass she retrieved from the floor.

"It was the first idea that jumped into my head. We could be going to the moon or to the movies, it doesn't matter. What we really want to do is go to bed."

Tracy set the glass down and studied Marisa intently. "I see," she said quietly.

"I can't hold him off any longer," Marisa said. "I don't want to hold him off any longer."

"You're in love with him."

Marisa closed her eyes. "I must be. I've never felt like this before, I can tell you that."

"Then sleep with him."

"Easy for you to say," Marisa replied distantly, without opening her eyes.

"What are you waiting for? You're a twenty-eight-year-old..."

"Please don't remind me," Marisa responded, looking at Tracy again. "That's the problem. How am I going to tell him?"

"Oh, I wouldn't worry too much on that score," Tracy said lightly, avoiding Marisa's gaze.

"Tracy, if we make love, he's going to figure it out. Trust me, he'll know."

"He won't care."

"How do you know? I've been working overtime to project the image of a mature, sophisticated woman, and I feel certain it will come as a bit of a shock to him to discover that he's in bed with Rebecca of Sunnybrook Farm."

"Maybe he'll think it's...charming."

"Maybe he'll think I'm retarded," Marisa said drearily.

"Come on."

"Repressed?" Marisa suggested.

"I doubt it."

"A social failure," Marisa concluded.

Tracy was sorely tempted to tell Marisa that Jack already knew, but she felt strongly that Jack had best handle that bulletin himself.

"Some men would feel flattered, that after being so selective for so long you chose him," she said reasonably.

"I'm not sure Jack falls into that category. Something tells me that while I was disecting cases and listening to tapes on Civil Procedure Jack was leaping from bed to bed like a hurdler."

"So what?"

"So I won't measure up to what he's used to. How could I?"

Tracy stood, dusting muffin crumbs from her lap onto the floor. "He doesn't want what he's used to. He wants you. Why can't you just accept that?"

"I don't know," Marisa mumbled, standing. "Seems too good to be true, I guess."

"Take the plunge, that's my advice. You're long overdue and this man is one in a million. If I were in your shoes I wouldn't hesitate."

Marisa smiled. "I know you wouldn't."

Tracy walked toward the connecting door of their rooms and then turned back to Marisa.

"But alas," she said, "he's not pursuing me. Well, I'll leave you to your deliberations. What's on the agenda for tomorrow?"

"Putting together the final figures on the cemetery removal."

"And in the evening, your hour of decision." She placed her hand dramatically over her heart.

"Go to bed, Tracy."

"Yes, boss." Tracy saluted and disappeared through the door.

Marisa lay down on the bed Tracy had vacated, trying to work up the energy to undress. She felt exhilarated and drained at the same time, which hardly seemed possible but was true, nevertheless. After a short while she turned off the bedside lamp and lay staring at the ceiling in the dark.

In two minutes she was asleep.

Jack sat back in the porch glider and stared up at the half moon hanging in the sky above the trees. Sleep was out of the question and the blank, glowing computer screen on the desk just inside the door was a mute reminder that he couldn't work, either. In fact, he hadn't been able to do anything at all since returning from his date with Marisa except think about her.

A loon called in the marsh beyond the border of his rental property, and the cry was answered by squawking nocturnal birds and humming insects. The Florida night was alive, and it made him feel less alone as he contemplated his life and his next move.

Jack had rented this isolated cabin, two miles in from the interstate on a dirt road, in order to have peace and quiet for his work. He had grown fond of the spot and had been thinking about buying the place when his six-month lease was up at the end of December. Of course, that might depend on how things went with Marisa. If they went any further at all.

Marisa was intelligent enough to know that they were at a crossroads; they weren't kids and the sexual tension between them was becoming unbearable. They were either going to do something about it or go their separate ways. He was alarmed to discover that he found the second possibility almost frightening.

Jack propped his feet up on the porch banister and the glider creaked with the movement. It was amazing how important this woman had become to him in such a short time. He found it difficult to concentrate on anything but his pursuit of her, and he didn't want to ruin his chances with her by taking the wrong step. He felt as uncertain as a schoolboy, but determined to have her anyway. For the first time in a long while he felt reckless and uncontrolled. If somebody tried to take her away from him now he'd fight for her.

Nobody had better get in his way. He stood purposefully and went back into the house.

Marisa dressed in a denim skirt and a flowered blouse for her date with Jack the next night. She was putting gold hoops in her ears when Tracy looked through the connecting door and groaned.

"Don't start," Marisa said warningly.

"That blouse buttons up to your eyeballs," Tracy said. "Don't you have anything with a scoop neck?"

"No."

"What are you wearing underneath?" Tracy asked.

Marisa threw her a disgusted glance.

"All right, all right. I always get lucky when I'm sporting the most ragged, ridiculous underwear I own. I was just trying to give you the benefit of my experience. It's best to be prepared," Tracy said. She disappeared briefly and then returned, proffering a hinged bangle bracelet set with tiny diamond chips.

"Wear this," she said. "For luck."

Marisa took the florentined ornament and clasped it around her wrist. "Thank you."

Tracy sighed. "I wish I were getting ready for a big date. The only men I've met down here are the gay doorman and Lasky's court clerk, who shows me pictures of his grandchildren."

"Your time will come."

"Not soon enough for me."

Marisa picked up her purse.

Tracy gave her a thumbs-up signal. "Win one for the gipper," she said.

Marisa was still smiling as she stepped off the elevator and saw Jack waiting in the lobby. He turned as if he sensed that she was there and his eyes met hers across the expanse that separated them. He was wearing a ribbed cotton sweater in a light maize color with tan cord jeans and leather boat shoes. When he moved toward her Marisa felt as if everyone else in the room had disappeared and left them alone together.

"Hi," he said softly.

"Hello."

"My car is parked in the underground garage," he said.

The gallery was on the other side of town, in a converted loft building near the developing suburbs. They parked across the street from it and approached the brightly lit exterior hand in hand. Marisa felt Jack hesitate when he saw that several of the militant young Indians who had picketed the courthouse were lounging in the doorway.

"Jack, this was a bad idea," she said quickly, stopping. "I just didn't think. You shouldn't be seen with me here. Let's go."

"The hell with that," he replied, his grip on her hand tightening as he tugged her along. "Come on."

Marisa inched closer to him and kept her eyes fixed on the ground as they approached the door. She felt the scrutiny of the onlookers, and then Jack shoved her behind him abruptly as one of the young men stepped into their path.

"Bluewolf," the youth said evenly.

"Forest," Jack replied in the same tone.

"I hope you're not planning to bring that lady inside," Jim Forest said, and there was no mistaking his sneering emphasis on the word "lady."

"Why not?" Jack said flatly. "I thought this gallery was open to the public."

"She's not the public. She's the enemy," Jim replied.

"Jim, you're confusing the issue," Jack said wearily. "Grow up before you open your mouth and make a fool of yourself again. Now let me by." Jack made as if to pass Jim and the latter shoved him, hard. Jack stumbled and Marisa gasped, putting her hand over her mouth.

"Jack, please," she begged, desperate to avoid an incident. Why on earth hadn't she guessed that something like this might happen? Jack had her so befuddled that she wasn't thinking clearly.

"Get your girlfriend out of here before something unpleasant happens to her," Jim said in a bullying tone.

"Nothing at all is going to happen to her," Jack said grimly, recovering his balance and grabbing Jim by the lapels of his jacket.

"Not as long as she has an apple like you running interference for her," Jim said, struggling in Jack's grip.

Jack's fist shot out so quickly that Jim was lying on the ground before Marisa knew what had happened.

"Get him out of here," Jack said tightly to Jim's companions, who were hovering uncertainly in the background, awaiting the outcome of the confrontation. They dragged the semiconscious boy to his feet and lugged him around the corner of the building.

"Jack, should we check and make sure he's all right?" Marisa asked anxiously.

"He'll survive, if the thickness of his intellect is any indication of the thickness of his skull," Jack replied, shaking the hand he had just used on Jim. Its knuckles were reddened and already beginning to swell.

"You shouldn't have hit him," Marisa said in dismay.

"Yes, I should. He's the worst of the bunch. He's been asking for somebody to take him down for a while. Unless I miss my guess it was his bright idea for Jeff Rivertree to shoot you. Jeff is just the gullible type to be used by a manipulator like Forest."

"What did he mean by calling you an apple?" Marisa asked.

"Red on the outside, white on the inside," Jack replied, glancing over at her.

"I see. That was a reference to me, then, to your choice of companions."

"That was a reference to his own idiocy. Nobody has the right to question my commitment to Indian affairs, least of all a layabout like Jim Forest, who hasn't done anything except run his mouth for the last ten years while I and a lot of other people have been working." Jack pushed his hair back off his forehead and then peered at Marisa intently. "Are you all right?" he asked.

"Of course not, Jack. This is awful. I would never want to be the source of trouble for you."

"You never could be."

"What do you call what just happened?"

"I call that a juvenile delinquent looking for an excuse to make trouble. The unfortunate thing about any cause, no matter how noble, is that a small lunatic fringe will be attracted to it for all the wrong reasons. Now let's take a stroll and look at the pictures."

"You don't mean you want to go inside after all?" Marisa asked him, aghast.

"I'm not going to let a lout like that drive me away,"
he said firmly, taking Marisa's hand again.

They were the objects of some staring once they
walked through the door, but after a while everybody
seemed to forget they were there. Jack stayed just long
enough to make his point, commenting on paintings
and sculpture and woven wall hangings while everything went past Marisa in a blur. She didn't draw a
comfortable breath until they were back out on the
street and heading for Jack's car.

"I'm glad that's over," she said as he unlocked her
door for her. "If I have any more bright ideas like that
one please institutionalize me until I regain my senses."

Jack walked around and slid onto the seat next to
her, then started the car.

"Why didn't you tell me to pick another destination
last night?" she asked him.

"You seemed to want to go to the gallery," he replied.

"I was just trying to think of someplace public where
we wouldn't . . ." she stopped short.

He let it pass.

"You must have guessed there might be trouble,"
Marisa said, after a pregnant pause.

"Well, I didn't know Jim Forest would be there.
That was just bad luck."

"Don't be evasive. Obviously your seeing me has not
been popular with your friends."

"They're not my friends."

"You know what I mean!"

"I do what I want," he said flatly. "If they can't
separate your professional duties from your personal
life, that's their problem, not mine."

Marisa saw that it was best to let the subject drop.

He looked over at her. "Where to?" he said, as he guided the car out into the street.

Marisa took a deep breath.

"I hear that the house where you're staying is in a very pretty spot," she said. "I'd like to see it."

Jack stopped for a traffic light and turned to look at Marisa, his arm across the back of the seat.

"Are you sure that's what you want?" he asked quietly, searching her face.

"Yes."

"Everything will be up to you," he added. "If you just want to visit and then go home, that will be fine."

Marisa nodded, her heart racing.

Jack turned left for the interstate and then drove for ten minutes before turning off onto a secondary road, then turning again onto an unpaved track which ran through scrub pines and citrus tress.

"It looks very...private," Marisa said nervously.

"It is. This is my second attempt in two days to take you to a remote area and then have my way with you."

When Marisa didn't reply, Jack looked over at her.

"Bad joke," he added ruefully.

Marisa said nothing.

Jack stopped the car and threw it into reverse.

"What are you doing?" Marisa asked, glancing around.

"You look like you're on your way to a funeral, which is not exactly the feeling I was hoping to inspire," he said dryly.

Marisa put her hand over his on the steering wheel.

"It's not you, Jack, it's me," she said quietly. "I have something to tell you."

"What is it?" he asked, looking at her intently, the car engine idling beneath them.

"Ah, this isn't easy to say."

"You've decided I'm the biggest jerk you've ever met."

"No, of course not."

"You got a telegram today from your doctor saying that you're dying of a rare disease."

"Don't joke about something like that," she said testily.

"Barring those two cases, nothing else matters." He gunned the motor forward again.

"But you don't understand . . ." she began.

"Yes, I do. We'll talk about it inside, all right?"

Marisa sighed and subsided. There was no reason to carry on this conversation in the car. He was right. It could wait.

They pulled into a clearing in front of an old-fashioned farmhouse with a wide porch and an oak paneled door. Marisa emerged from the car to find that an evening breeze had sprung up, rustling the trees surrounding them and providing a counterpoint to the calls of the nightbirds from the marsh.

"This is so lovely, Jack," she said, following him onto the wooden steps.

"Yeah, it's been a great place to work. It's part of an estate. The daughter lives up north and doesn't want it, so the lawyer handling the will is trying to unload it."

"Have you been thinking of buying it?"

"I'd like to," he said, unlocking the door, "but I'm not sure it would be worth the money. I don't know how often I'd be able to get here."

"After the case is over, you mean."

He turned to look at her as he switched on the light. "Yes. I won't be in Florida much longer."

On that cheerful note, Marisa walked into the living room, which ran the width of the house. There was a fieldstone fireplace which took up most of one wall, a large rag rug on the floor in front of it, and rustic native pine furniture filling the open space. Through the doorway she could see a vintage kitchen and, behind it, a stairwell ascending to the second floor. Where the bedrooms were, she supposed.

"It's getting chilly, would you like a fire?" Jack asked.

"Don't go to any trouble."

"No trouble, it's all set. I just have to put a match to it." He picked up a pack of matches from the mantel and struck one, then lit the crumpled newspapers folded against the wrought iron screen. Marisa watched as they smoldered and caught fire, the flames licking the logs piled on top of them.

"There, it will be warm in a few minutes. This house is built like a hospital, with cross-ventilation. It's always cool, a real advantage in Florida. The old guy who designed it knew what he was doing. He built most of this furniture, too." He gathered up a stack of papers from the love seat in front of the fireplace and added, "Have a seat."

Marisa sat down.

"Do you want a drink? Coffee or tea?"

Marisa shook her head.

He clapped his hands together. "Well, I'm running out of small talk. How about those Dolphins?"

Marisa smiled thinly.

He came and sat next to her. "What is it?" he said.

Marisa looked at him, so handsome, so desirable, his face alive with intelligence and concern. With a sound like a sob she flung her arms around his neck.

"Hey, hey," he said gently, his arms coming around her immediately. "Take it easy. I'm not forcing anything on you. I'll take you back to the hotel right now if..."

"I do want you, I do," she whispered fiercely, interrupting him. "So much."

"You got me, babe. Here I am."

Marisa drew back and fingered the cabling around the neck of his sweater.

"There's something you have to know," she said slowly.

"I think I already know," he replied.

Marisa stared at him.

"I know that you're a...beginner."

"Beginner?" Marisa said slowly.

"With men."

Marisa closed her eyes as the blood rushed into her face. "Has it been that obvious?" she said in an agonized whisper, finding that possibility unbearable.

"Of course not. In fact, I thought just the opposite until Tracy told me."

"I'll kill her," Marisa said, not opening her eyes.

"Don't feel that way. She did us both a favor."

Marisa still couldn't look at him.

"I was about to give up on you," he said earnestly. "She made your behavior understandable and gave me some hope, don't you see that?" He tucked a tendril of her hair behind her ear and her lashes lifted.

"You must have been laughing at me all this while," she said miserably.

He pulled her back into his arms. "Sweetheart, no. I admit that at first I could hardly believe it."

"Thanks a lot."

"But when I had time to think about it, some of the things you had done became..."

"Less idiotic?" she supplied.

"More reasonable."

"I'm surprised you didn't run screaming for the trees."

"Why would I do that? It just convinced me that what I had suspected from the beginning was true."

"That I'm stunted?"

"That you're a very special person."

"Oh, Jack." She hugged him tighter, and when he turned his head and kissed her she responded with all her heart.

Jack slipped his arm under her legs and lifted her bodily onto the love seat, so that she was lying across his lap. Her mouth opened under his and she tasted his tongue as he kissed her deeply. She ran her hands down his back, slipping them under his sweater to touch his bare skin. Jack groaned and pressed her down into the cushions as she sank her fingers into the thick, blade straight hair at the back of his neck. His lips traveled to her throat and he pushed her collar aside impatiently. His hand fumbled with the buttons on her blouse and he muttered an oath.

"What?" she said.

"I can't do this, I'm shaking," he said, exasperated.

"Oh, look at your poor hand," Marisa said, sitting up and seizing it. "Shouldn't we put some ice on that?"

"Now? Are you kidding?" he said, staring at her.

"That's the second injury you've suffered because of me," Marisa mourned, kissing the abraded knuckles.

"Forget it," he said. "Let's do it this way." He yanked the loosened blouse out of her skirt band and pulled it over her head. In almost the same motion he doffed his sweater and swept her back into his arms.

"Oh, Marisa, you're like velvet, all over," he said huskily, his cheek against her hair. He undid the clasp of her bra with a stout yank and tossed it on the floor.

"I think I ripped it," he said into her ear.

"Who cares?" Marisa responded, gasping as her naked flesh met his once more. She ran the palms of her hands up his arms and rested them on either side of his neck. He drew back to look at her face, and then dropped his eyes.

"Am I the first man to see this?" he said softly.

"There's not much to see," Marisa replied, almost shrinking under his penetrating gaze.

"You're beautiful, perfect," he replied, bending and taking a pink-tan nipple in his mouth. Marisa sucked in her breath and held his head against her. He shifted position until he was kneeling on the floor in front of her, moving back and forth. Marisa wrapped her arms around his shoulders and surrendered to his caresses.

When he looked up, his mouth swollen and his eyes vacant with pleasure, Marisa touched his face tenderly.

"Yes?" he asked.

"Yes," she answered.

He pulled a folded quilt from the back of the love seat and spread it on the floor. Then he put his arms around her waist and pulled her down to join him. They lay full-length for a long moment, Marisa watching the play of the firelight on his cheekbones as he loomed above her, his dark eyes filling the world.

"I've wanted you from the first moment I saw you," Jack said huskily. "That first day in court, you were wearing a dark blue dress with silver buttons down the front, and ankle strap shoes. Do you remember?"

"I remember."

"And silver earrings, like stars."

"Did you take a picture?"

"The picture is in my head," he said, bending to kiss her again. This time there was no mistaking the urgency in his manner; very shortly, there would be no turning back. When he reached for the zipper on her skirt Marisa stiffened.

"What?" he said.

"A little nervous, I guess."

"I'll take it slow, I promise." He removed the skirt and embraced her again, turning so that they lay side by side. Wearing nothing but her thin briefs, Marisa buried her face in his shoulder, touching his scab with her fingers.

"Does this hurt?" he murmured.

"Not anymore."

She kissed the wound, then traced the outline of his collarbone with her lips. He fell back, watching her, as she drew her mouth across his chest, tonguing first his nipples, then the line of dark hair which descended toward his waist. He rubbed the back of her head with his hand, and then, as she explored his navel, he made an inarticulate sound and seized her almost roughly, flipping her onto her back and enveloping her with his body.

"Now," he said urgently.

"I'm ready," she replied.

She watched as he stood, unbuckling his belt and stripping off the rest of his clothes. When he joined her again he held her in the curve of one arm and tugged on her panties impatiently. When the material resisted he ripped the briefs free of her limbs with one tight motion and tossed them aside, mounting her.

"I'll buy you another set, all silk," he said into her ear.

"I don't care," she replied, sighing as she felt him, full and ready, against her. He lifted himself off her with one arm and ran his free hand between her legs. Marisa moaned and closed her eyes.

"Are you sure?" he asked, his muscles trembling with the effort of restraining himself.

"I'm sure," she whispered, gasping as he stroked the sensitive flesh. "Please, I'm sure."

He settled into position and she wrapped her legs around his narrow hips.

"This . . . it may hurt," he gasped.

Marisa pulled him tighter.

When he entered her Marisa stiffened and he stopped immediately.

"All right?" he said hoarsely.

She said something in a low tone, her voice muffled against the side of his neck.

"What?" he whispered.

"More," she said.

He gave her more.

When Jack awoke a few hours later, the fire was dying and Marisa was gone. He got up, slipping on his jeans, and added a couple of logs to replenish the blaze. Then he padded barefoot into the kitchen where he found Marisa, seated at the deal table and sipping a cup of tea. She was wearing his plaid bathrobe, which reached to her ankles and came down over her wrists.

With her wavy blond hair and oversize outfit she looked like Shirley Temple in *Little Miss Marker*.

"Are you all right?" he asked.

"Never been better."

"Do you need to use the bathroom?" he asked anxiously.

"Already found it. This," she indicated the robe, "was hanging on the back of the door."

"And you're okay?" he repeated.

Marisa smiled. "Jack, I've been deflowered, not shot. I assure you, I'm fine."

He bent over her and lifted the trailing hair off her neck, kissing her nape. "Why didn't you wake me?"

"You were sleeping so soundly, I didn't want to disturb you."

He slipped into a chair across from her, sliding down until he was resting on his spine.

"I was enjoying the sleep of the satisfied. I wasn't sleeping so well before tonight."

"Were you tormented by thoughts of me, poor boy?" Marisa asked teasingly.

"I was," he said seriously, holding her gaze.

The silence lengthened between them as Marisa felt her mouth going dry.

Jack got up and took her hand.

"Want to try the bed this time?" he said.

Marisa rose and followed him to the stairs.

The telephone rang at seven-thirty the next morning. Jack fumbled for it with his free hand as Marisa raised her head from his shoulder.

"Yeah?" he growled. He listened for a second and then handed the phone to Marisa.

"For you," he said and fell back on the pillow.

"H'lo," Marisa said.

"News flash," Tracy announced. "That creep from the Indian Affairs Bureau is back again, and he wants to see you. Today."

"Randall Block?"

"The very same."

"How did you know where to find me?" Marisa asked, her head beginning to clear.

"Wild guess," Tracy replied dryly. "I got the number from Ben Brady. After a struggle, I might add."

"All right. I'll be there as soon as I can make it."

"Did the big event take place?" Tracy asked eagerly.

"I'll tell you about it later," Marisa replied.

"Spoilsport," Tracy observed. "I'll see you soon. And I mean soon. I can't handle this guy alone. 'Bye."

"Goodbye." Marisa hung up the receiver and collapsed onto Jack's chest.

"Don't tell me. You have to work today."

"Right the first time."

"You grab a shower and I'll make the coffee," he said, sliding out of bed.

"I'll have to sneak past the doorman. I'll be wearing the same clothes I wore last night," Marisa observed, wrapping herself in the sheet.

"Not to mention no underwear," he replied, grinning.

"That's right, it's in shreds," she groaned.

"The doorman will have a treat."

"I don't think so. He's gay."

"I'm not." He pulled the sheet off Marisa and tumbled her onto the bed.

"I have to hurry," she protested. Feebly.

"I can hurry," he answered, pressing her back into the mattress.

"What about the coffee?"

"We'll pick it up at the convenience store on the way into town," he murmured, nibbling her neck.

"Oh, all right." She sighed, and surrendered.

# Six

"So what's up with Randall Blockhead?" Tracy greeted Marisa when she entered the hotel suite that afternoon.

Marisa dropped her briefcase on the bed and shook her head. "He's very displeased with me," she said dryly.

"Do tell."

"I am not winning the case, that's clear, and what's worse, I have not reached an 'accommodation' with the Seminoles."

"What the hell does that mean?"

"It means he wants this over, that's what it means. It's dragging on forever, much longer than anticipated. Ben Brady is throwing up every obstacle he can concoct, which is costing the feds a fortune. All of this I heard from Mr. Block's lips, as if I didn't already know it."

"What does he expect from you, a miracle?"

"Evidently. I told him if they had found someone who could do a better job I would be happy to turn over all my materials to that person and go home, humming all the way."

"What did he say?"

"Nothing, of course. The problem with this situation isn't the lawyer, it's the case. We haven't got one, not one good enough to snatch that burial ground from people who've had it for hundreds of years. Block knows it. He's just taking out his frustrations on me. I let him do that for a while and then I came back here."

"Sounds like a fun time," Tracy said gloomily.

"But there is good news," Marisa said, grinning suddenly. Tracy looked at her and brightened.

"How did it go with Jack?" she asked, favoring Marisa with a sly, sidelong glance.

"Marvelously, stupendously, sublimely. And aside from that, it was wonderful." Marisa sat in a chair and sighed blissfully.

"I'm jealous," Tracy announced.

The telephone rang. Tracy answered it on the first ring, listened, and then held it out to Marisa.

"Guess who?" she said.

Marisa leaped up and snatched the phone from Tracy's grasp. "Hello?" she said breathlessly.

"How's my girl?" Jack asked.

"Happy."

"Glad to hear it. Are you finished with your lawyer stuff for the day?"

"Looks like it."

"Good. I'll pick you up at seven."

"What are we doing?"

"Oh, we'll think of something." The line went dead.

"Well?" Tracy inquired expectantly, as Marisa moved to hang up the phone.

"He's coming for me in a couple of hours."

"I guess I won't be seeing much of you in the evenings now," Tracy observed.

"Well, once we go back into court next week I won't have much free time. I thought I'd take advantage of the chance to spend time with him while I can."

"Oh, don't explain, I understand. It's just...I don't know anybody in this burg and I've appreciated your company."

"And I've appreciated yours," Marisa replied warmly.

They regarded each other in silence for a minute.

"Okay," Tracy said briskly, "before we burst into tears here, I'm going down to the pharmacy for toothpaste. Do you want anything?"

"No, thanks."

"See you later." Tracy went out and Marisa walked over to the closet to see what she had to wear for that evening.

When Marisa left her room to meet Jack she found him waiting outside the elevator on her floor.

"What are you doing here?" she asked, laughing, as he swept her into his arms.

"I got impatient waiting in the lobby, so I thought I'd come up, but then I didn't want to burst in on you with Tracy there. So I compromised with this."

"You're very silly, do you know that?" Marisa murmured into his collar.

"All part of my charm," he replied, holding her off to examine her intently.

"What?"

"I wanted to see if you looked any different," he said teasingly.

"From this morning?"

"It's been ten hours."

"Ten hours, twenty-two minutes and thirteen seconds," Marisa corrected him.

"Ah, you've been counting, too." He drew her back into his embrace and said in her ear, "Let's get out of here."

It was a quiet drive out to his house. They were both thinking the same thing. Once they arrived they went wordlessly up the stairs and into Jack's bedroom. He took the receiver off the hook and smothered it with a pillow.

"Come here," he said. He unbuttoned her blouse and took off her slacks, smiling when he saw the lace teddy underneath them.

"What's this?" he asked.

"One-piece underwear," she replied. "Very efficient."

"Why wear any at all?" he said huskily, separating the garment from her skin.

"Juries might find it a little peculiar," she replied.

"Not to mention stimulating."

"And the judges? They're usually men."

"I'm sure your win rate would go up." He bent to mouth her breast and then picked her up and put her in the bed. She lay back against the pillows and held out her arms.

Jack doffed his clothes in seconds, kicking off his jeans so hard that they flew into a corner.

"Take it easy," Marisa said, giggling.

"Not a chance." He dove on top of her, flinging the sheet to the foot of the bed.

"Ah, that's better," she said, sighing. "You feel so good."

"And soon I'll feel even better," he said in her ear, and proceeded to prove it.

Marisa snuggled into the solid warmth of Jack's shoulder and looked around the dimly lit room. Books were piled on makeshift shelves in two corners, stacked randomly and leaning crazily against one another. A portable television sat atop a cabinet which stored a set of free weights and a tape deck with a pile of tapes wedged in next to it. Jack's toiletries in the bathroom, his clothes in the closet and the computer on the first floor were the only other personal items in the house.

"You must get tired of setting up camp in places like this for a few weeks or a few months at a time," Marisa said. "Don't you ever want a more permanent home?"

"I guess that's Oklahoma, if where my family lives is home."

"How old are you?"

"Thirty-five. How old are you?" She could tell by the sound of his voice in the dark that he was smiling.

"Twenty-eight."

"Now that we have exchanged that important information, is there anything else you want to know? What diseases I've had, what I've been innoculated against, the number of my caps and crowns?"

"Don't make fun of me. I was just thinking that all this has happened so fast. I don't really know that much about you."

He propped a pillow behind his head and sat up, pulling her with him. "What else do you want to know? What I did on my first date?"

Marisa sighed, recognizing that she was encountering a familiar male attitude: the past is over, why talk about it?

"You could start there," she said.

"I went to the movies with Mary Beth Reynolds," he said. "We saw *Love Story* at the Rialto, ate two tubs of popcorn and a box of Milk Duds candy. Mary Beth cried so hard during the death scene that her contact lenses washed out of her eyes."

"Sounds like a dream date."

"Actually, except for the contacts, it wasn't bad. Mary Beth and I hit it off and wound up going together for the next couple of years. She was living at a neighboring girls' school and we saw each other almost every weekend."

"What happened?"

"Oh, her parents broke it up. Cochise was not exactly what they had in mind for their little princess. Six years later she married an orthopedic surgeon and had three kids. I just heard a few months ago that he recently left her for his college-age receptionist."

"Sounds like you've kept up."

"Oh, she saw my picture in the paper when I spoke at a college near where she lives and she wrote me a letter through the NFN."

"Trying to fan the old flame?" Marisa suggested.

He shifted position to look at her. "Why, Miss Hancock, I do believe you're jealous."

"Would it be so strange if I were?" she replied, putting her arms around his neck and kissing him.

"I think I like it," he said against her mouth, pulling her down into the bed with him.

And that was the end of the conversation.

\* \* \*

When Marisa awoke, the room was as dark as a cave. It took her several seconds to identify the sound she heard as running water, and then she realized that Jack was taking a shower. She lay there, pleasantly satiated, until the door to the bathroom opened, revealing a yellow slip of light for a second before Jack snapped off the switch. He came out, barefoot and silent, toweling his hair, moving carefully so he didn't have to turn on another light.

"What time is it?" she asked drowsily.

"Ah, you're awake. It's ten-thirty." He sat on the edge of the bed next to her.

"You smell wonderful," she said, reaching her bare arms up to encircle his neck.

He laughed. "It's soap." He snapped on the bedside lamp.

"Soap and you, that's different." She hugged him for a long moment and then said, as an afterthought, "I'm hungry."

He grinned. "I'm not surprised."

"Is there anything downstairs?" Marisa asked, rolling over and feeling on the floor for her clothes.

"I don't remember. I'll take a look." Jack slid off the bed and into his jeans as Marisa headed for the bathroom.

"I'll be down in a couple of minutes," she called after him.

The bathroom had a modern stall shower, obviously a recent addition, and as Marisa adjusted the nozzle and stepped under the spray she examined the shampoo and other items stashed in the hanging mesh rack. It did not seem odd to be in his house or his bed. She didn't know what that meant, but it was true.

When she was through, she dried off on one of Jack's huge bath towels and dressed haphazardly in her slacks with her blouse tied loosely at the waist. Then she followed him down to the kitchen, blinking in the harsh overhead light.

"I feel like a Morlock," she said.

"A hungry one," he replied, opening the refrigerator.

"Yes. What have we got to eat?"

"Well, let's see. In here we have ketchup, pickles, three grapefruits, an onion, and a bottle of mineral water."

"Mmm."

He turned and pulled open a cupboard above her head. "And in here we have crackers, mayonnaise, potato buds and oatmeal."

"Yech."

"I have been eating out a lot."

"So it would seem."

"There's a Chinese place about three miles away that stays open late, and delivers," he suggested.

"Oh, good. Then I won't have to get dressed up."

"I'm in favor of that," he replied, rummaging in a drawer. He held out a takeout menu for her to see.

"I knew I had this someplace," he said triumphantly.

"Shanghai Sam's?" she said, reading the heading.

"Despite the name, the food is good."

"What's that interesting stain on the edge of the menu?" Marisa asked, laughing.

"Moo goo gai pan?" he said.

"Don't ask me."

"Probably chicken lo mein," he amended. "That's always been a favorite of mine. What would you like?"

"Anything. I'm in no mood to be particular."

He lifted the receiver of the wall phone and frowned. "It seems to be dead."

"It's off the hook upstairs," Marisa reminded him.

"Oh, right. Would you go up and replace it?"

Marisa did so.

"Do they know you at Shanghai Sam's?" Marisa asked, grinning, as she reentered the kitchen.

"I am the best customer of Shanghai Sam's. Also of Bay Point Pizza, Mabel's Lunch, and Uncle Morty's Subs." He tossed the menu back in the drawer and slammed it shut.

"Not to mention Leduc's, and that sawdust wonderland we patronized the other night."

"Correct."

"I gather you don't like to cook."

"I can't cook, there's a difference. I have tried. Everything always winds up burned, dried, flattened, or whatever it's not supposed to be. I gave up a long time ago." He extended his arms invitingly and she walked into them.

"I suppose you can cook, of course," he said, nestling his cheek against her hair.

"A little. I'm no chef."

"I ordered shrimp in lobster sauce with saffron rice and sautéed string beans."

"Sounds good."

"Low sodium, no MSG," he added.

Marisa drew back to look at him.

"That's what it says on the menu," he said, shrugging. He undid the knot at her waist carefully and pulled back her shirttails to reveal her bare midriff.

"Jack," Marisa said warningly.

"Yes?" He bent to plant a kiss on her skin just above the button on her slacks.

"Someone is going to be delivering that order in about five minutes," she said.

"Ten."

"What's the difference? I need sustenance, Jack, I'm not used to this pace."

"Are you suggesting that I'm wearing you out?" he said.

"If I faint, it's your fault," she said impishly, slipping out of his grasp.

"Oh, all right. I suppose I do have to feed you." He got a couple of glasses out of another cupboard and rinsed them under the tap.

"Jack?"

"Yeah?" He looked over his shoulder at her.

"What's going to happen when all this is over?" she asked.

"All what?" He put the glasses on the table.

"The case, you know."

"We'll go on as before," he said lightly, not looking at her

"But I live in Maine, for heaven's sake."

"So what? It's not the moon. There are planes and trains and roads that go there, right?"

"Do you mean that?" she said quietly.

"Of course. Did you imagine that I would leave here and forget you?" he asked, taking napkins from a box on the counter.

"I . . . I didn't know."

"Come here," he said, putting the napkins down.

Marisa stepped into his arms again.

"What do you think, that this is a casual fling for me?" he said gently, stroking her hair.

"I was hoping not."

"But you were still willing to take the chance?"

"I wanted you, Jack. But I knew you must have done this sort of thing before," she said lamely.

"Not this sort of thing," he said quietly.

The doorbell rang.

"Saved by the bell?" Marisa said.

"Don't make light of it," he said soberly, releasing her. "I meant what I said." He went to answer the door and when he returned he was carrying two brown bags and a newspaper.

"I forgot to take this off the steps," he said, putting the paper aside and diving into one of the bags.

Marisa went to join him, postponing the subject of their relationship until later.

"Can you use these?" he asked, indicating the set of wooden chopsticks included with his order. He took the mineral water out of the refrigerator and filled their glasses.

"Hold one stick like a pencil," Marisa said, demonstrating.

Jack sat down, opened a carton, and attempted to imitate her. A shrimp slid into his lap.

"Thank you," he said, staring down at his jeans.

"You asked."

"Stop showing off," he added, as she manipulated the chopsticks dexterously.

"I'd advise you to get a fork, Jackson," Marisa commented, grinning wickedly.

He went for some silverware and sat again, saying, "It must be genetic. Native Americans aren't meant to use those things."

"I'm no more Chinese than you are."

He used his fork as a slingshot and sent a string bean flying in her direction.

"That was mature," Marisa said.

"My specialty, maturity."

"So I've noticed." Marisa opened the newspaper and riffled through the pages.

"You're not reading the newspaper tonight," he said, around a mouthful of rice.

"It says here that *Deception* is playing on the movie channel at twelve o'clock."

"You're not watching television tonight," he added.

"Oh, come on! It's a great movie, Bette Davis at the top of her form. Terrific music, too."

"I can't watch that—those shoulder pads she wears are too distracting."

"You're thinking of Joan Crawford."

"I am not. Crawford is the one with the bug eyes and Davis is the one who's always spinning around, flipping her skirts. And smoking."

"They're both always smoking. I can see you're really a fan of forties movies."

"They're so dated, aren't they? And the dialogue, so corny!"

"That's part of their nostalgic appeal, something a writer should be able to appreciate. And Davis is really good in this one." Marisa popped the last string bean in her mouth and chewed industriously.

"I feel I should warn you that if you're addicted to Bette Davis weepers, the future of this relationship is in doubt."

"Watch out or I'll tie you down and force you to watch *Dark Victory* with me."

"Which one is that?"

"Bette is a playgirl with a brain tumor who falls in love with her doctor."

"Spare me. I thought you didn't like television."

"I don't, not today's television. I like old movies, pre-nineteen-sixty, preferably." She smiled invitingly. "We could build a fire and watch it together on that old console TV in the living room."

"How about the portable in the bedroom?" he said, grinning.

"Not a chance. I want to see the film, Jack."

He shrugged. "I'm sure it'll be better than the programs on the tube. The only television I really watch is CNN and sometimes the sports channel, anyway."

"Liar. You're probably addicted to Saturday morning cartoons."

"Well, I am partial to Scooby Doo."

"I knew it!"

He scraped the bottom of the rice carton and tossed the empty container in the trash.

"But in all honesty I'd have to say I'm equally fond of Spiderman," he added, smiling.

"Hah! And I'll bet you watch the shopping channel all night and buy onyx rings at three o'clock in the morning."

"I confess that when I've been up late with a manuscript I've had it on occasionally. Some of those people who call in during the wee hours really do bear watching."

Marisa looked at the wall clock pointedly. "I rest my case. Bette's waiting."

"You owe me one." He rose, grumbling, and Marisa heard him laying a fire in the living room as she straightened the kitchen. By the time she joined him the movie was on and he was using the bellows on the fire to get it going.

"Isn't that the guy from that Ingrid Bergman flick?" he asked, gesturing at the screen.

"That's Claude Rains. He was in every Ingrid Bergman movie. And every Bette Davis movie, too, I think." Marisa settled on the couch and turned up the volume slightly.

"No, no, you know the one I mean, the famous one. Humphrey Bogart in North Africa, World War II?"

"You are referring, I believe, to *Casablanca?*"

"Right. This guy was the crooked police chief or something?" Jack put the bellows back on the rack and stood up.

"Yes. He's a symphony conductor in this one."

Jack sat next to her and folded his arms behind his head. "And how about the one where he's a neo-Nazi married to Ingrid and Cary Grant is the government agent?"

Marisa stared at him. "I thought you hated old movies."

"I never said that. I said they were dated and corny, but I've seen my share of them."

"Apparently."

"I'm a night owl. I do a lot of my writing late at night. If I get stuck I sometimes turn on the TV. That's when they're on, okay?"

"You would never be caught renting one, of course."

"Of course." He leaned forward to adjust the color knob. "I guess this one hasn't been 'colorized,'" he said, when the picture remained black and white.

"Thank God. I saw the colorized version of *Little Women* and everything and everybody in it was sepia, like those daguerreotypes from the Civil War."

He chuckled.

"Who's this?" he inquired, as the screen featured a close-up.

"Paul Henreid."

"Looks familiar."

"Ingrid's husband in *Casablanca*," Marisa said dryly.

He snapped his fingers. "Right!"

Marisa shot him a sidelong glance as he settled back and fixed his gaze on the screen.

"What?" he said, looking at her.

"I thought you were enduring this for my sake."

"Well?"

"Don't look too much like you're enjoying yourself or I might get the wrong impression."

He reached out suddenly and yanked her into his lap.

"Forget Paul whatever his name is. He's dead. I'm right here and I'm alive."

"So I see."

He untied her blouse and eased the sleeves off her arms.

"What about the movie?" she asked.

"We'll just have to watch it another time," he replied, unbuttoning her slacks.

The screen flickered in the background as they made love.

In the morning Marisa woke to find herself in Jack's bed, having no recollection of getting there. She slipped into a shirt she found lying on the dresser and padded downstairs barefoot, to find him scrambling eggs in the kitchen as the delicious smell of brewing coffee wafted around him.

"Good morning, gorgeous," he said, saluting her enthusiastically with a spatula.

"I thought you couldn't cook," she said, putting her arms around his waist from behind as he stood at the stove.

"This is the limit of my repertoire," he replied, leaning back into her embrace.

"How did I get upstairs last night?" she asked, opening the refrigerator to discover it stocked with new items.

"How do you think? I carried you."

"And when did you buy all this stuff?" she asked, removing a carton of cream from the refrigerator and putting it on the table.

"I got up early and went to the store."

"You must think I have a big appetite," she said, laughing.

"I *know* you have a big appetite, darlin'," he answered, grinning wickedly.

"Stop making fun of me. You started me on the path to destruction," Marisa replied.

Jack turned off the burner on the stove and carried the pan to the table. It was already set with dishes and cutlery, and a plate of toast sat in the middle of it.

Marisa selected a piece and bit into it.

"Not bad," she said optimistically.

"Liar. I burned it."

"Only slightly. I hate pale toast anyway."

"You won't get that around here, mine is always charred." He scooped the eggs onto her plate and then sat across from her, watching as she took a sample.

"Very good," she said brightly.

He took a bit himself.

"Not bad, if I do say so," he agreed, digging in with relish. "So, what are we going to do today?"

"Jack, I have to work."

"Come on, you can play hooky for one day."

"I don't think so," Marisa said. "I didn't come to Florida to socialize with you, Jackson, I came to represent a client."

"Socialize?" he said, raising his brows. "Is that what we've been doing?"

"If you're going to take a double meaning from everything I say, I'm going to stop talking to you."

"As long as you don't stop sleeping with me," he said, shoveling a forkful of eggs into his mouth.

She kicked him under the table.

"Ow. You're on a break from court now. Can't whatever you have to do wait until tomorrow?"

Marisa hesitated, sorely tempted.

"You're a bad influence," she finally said.

"So I've been told," he replied.

"What about you? Don't you have writing to do?"

"It can wait."

"We're both going to wind up unemployed," Marisa said gloomily, munching toast.

Jack got up and took her hand, leading her out of her chair and into his arms.

"Let's take this time while we have the chance," he said against her hair. "It may be difficult for us to get together in the future."

Marisa felt a chill. What was he trying to say?

"We'll find a way, won't we?" she said anxiously.

"Of course we will. But this interlude is a gift. Let's take advantage of it while we can."

"All right," Marisa said, looking up at him.

"I have an idea."

"Somehow I thought you might."

"My friend who owns the boat also has a beach house."

"What is this guy, a millionaire?"

"He's well off, yeah."

"Why doesn't he keep his boat at the beach?"

"You can't dock a boat on the open ocean, it would get battered to pieces. Are you sure you live in Maine?"

"I forgot," she said sheepishly. "So what about the beach house? And I think I should warn you that, despite your recent swimming escapades, the water here is a bit too chilly for me."

"So we won't swim. The view is beautiful. We'll walk on the beach, take a lunch along with us, okay?"

"Okay," Marisa said, ducking her head against his shoulder and clutching him tightly.

It was sunny when they left the house. Twenty minutes later it was overcast, and by the time they got to the beach it was pouring rain. They trudged through the wet sand and climbed up the exterior stairs to the deck, and then Jack unlocked the sliding glass doors. They bustled through them and turned glumly to watch the rivulets of water running down the glass, obscuring the shoreline in a gray wash.

"So, this was a great idea, huh?" Jack said flatly, and Marisa laughed.

"I'm not a weatherman," he said, shrugging. "Sue me."

"I wouldn't dream of it." Marisa flung herself on him and they both tumbled onto the suede couch to the left of the door.

"Who needs sunshine?" he said.

"Not us." They lay together and listened to the rain drumming on the roof of the A-frame house. "Why does your friend do for a living?" Marisa asked. "This place reeks of money."

"Actually, he doesn't do much. I think he inherited most of it. His father invented something and it's kept them all in the chips for about fifty years."

"What did his father invent?"

"Some kind of aquarium cover."

Marisa sat up, staring down at him. "An aquarium cover?" she said incredulously.

"I'm serious. It allows the fish to breathe, or be fed through it, or something. Pet stores and zoos use it. I'm telling you, the thing was a big hit."

Marisa started to giggle, and then laughed out loud. "The house the fish feeder built," she said, gesturing to the walls.

"This ain't the half of it, honey. You haven't seen the family house in Jacksonville, the co-op in New York, or the flat in Paris."

"How did you meet this guy?"

"School," he said, offhandedly.

"Oh. The prep school where you didn't fit in too well."

"That's the one."

"And he befriended you."

"How do you know it wasn't the other way around?"

"Well, he would have felt secure in that environment, so it stands to reason he'd be the one sticking up for you. Am I right?"

"You know a lot about human nature, don't you?" he said, pulling her down next to him again.

Marisa shrugged, embarrassed.

"You're right," Jack said. "He did help me a lot. He was my roommate in college, too. It was his wife you saw me with in the hotel dining room that night we…"

"Made fools of ourselves?" Marisa suggested.

He grinned. "You were jealous, weren't you? When you thought she was my date."

"I was not," Marisa said indignantly, snuggling into his side and sighing contentedly.

"Tell the truth."

"Well, maybe a little."

He chuckled.

"Aren't you pleased with yourself? That's exactly what you were trying to accomplish, right?"

"I was having dinner with a friend, give me a break!"

"You knew what I would think, and that's precisely what you wanted me to think. You could at least be honest about it."

He threw his head back and closed his eyes. "Oh, all right, all right. I was trying to make you jealous. Are you happy now?"

"Very childish of you, Jackson."

"Yes, I know. But effective. I knew you needed a little push in the right direction, and I supplied it."

"You knew?"

"I hoped."

"That's better." Marisa rolled over and looked at the ceiling. "What are all those little caps up there?" she asked, pointing.

"Recessed lighting."

"Please. I may not be the editor of *Architectural Digest,* but I've seen recessed lighting. That's not it."

"I'm serious. You press one of those white buttons over there on the wall and all the little caps open up, and lights emerge on aluminum stalks, like in a science fiction movie."

Marisa propped herself up on one elbow and looked at him, eyebrows raised.

"Try it," he said.

Marisa jumped up and ran to the panel he had indicated. She pressed the top button and the floor-length drapes swooshed closed across the glass doors.

"Wrong button," Jack said from the couch, unnecessarily.

She pressed the second button, and a television set emerged from the wall next to the fireplace.

"It's the third one down on the left," Jack said, in a tone of exaggerated patience.

Marisa located the right button, and all the ceiling caps receded simultaneously to a low whirring sound.

"Look at that," she said in amazement. "Does your friend have an aversion to track lighting?"

"His father doesn't like to see lamps during the daytime, when he doesn't need them."

"Eccentric millionaires," Marisa sighed. "What does the rest of this place look like?"

"I will be happy to provide a tour," Jack said, standing and throwing his arms wide.

Marisa scurried to fall into step beside him.

"On your right," he said, in the ringing tones of a museum guide, "you will find the space-age kitchen, complete with trash compactor, double stainless steel sink, and walk-in refrigerator."

"Who needs a walk-in refrigerator? Is somebody studying forensic medicine?"

"Don't interrupt the guide," Jack said.

"Sorry."

"Pantry," Jack said, gesturing with one hand, "and laundry room," he added, gesturing with the other.

"Very impressive."

Jack walked across the glazed tile floor to indicate the dining room, which featured a pegged pine floor, a dazzling art deco chandelier, and a hand-knotted rug which looked as if it were loomed the day before it settled on the gleaming boards.

"Just a trifle nouveau riche, don't you think, Jackson?" Marisa asked, sniffing.

"I don't know about the nouveau, but definitely riche." He made a sweeping gesture toward the living room they had just vacated. "And you saw the rest in there, the matched skin couches and chairs, the Mexican marble cocktail tables, the natural stone fireplace, the Jackson Pollock on the wall."

"I have only one question," Marisa said.

"Yes?"

"Where's the bedroom?"

He crooked his finger. "Follow me."

The open spiral staircase led to a second floor loft and a series of guest rooms down the hall. There was another fireplace on the exterior wall of the loft and a second deck overlooking the ocean.

"Nice digs," she commented.

"It's okay, if you like luxury," Jack replied.

The loft was furnished with a vintage Shaker set with a peg post king bed, bleached pine end tables and a standing armoire. The bathroom leading off it had a Jacuzzi tub and an oversize shower stall with a frosted glass enclosure.

"Come back here," Jack called, as Marisa disappeared through the door.

She came back and stood in the doorway.

"Let's see if this mattress works," he said.

She ran and jumped up on him, and they fell on top of the down comforter.

"What's this you're wearing?" he asked, tugging on her collar impatiently.

"It's called a blouse. You remember it, you took it off me last night, too."

He unbuttoned it efficiently and threw it on the floor.

"So much for that," she said, sighing.

He disposed of the rest of her clothes in the same manner and then lay next to her, tracing the line of her hip with his forefinger.

"Is this a physical?" she said. "Should I have brought my insurance information?"

He bent and took her nipple in his mouth.

"I guess not," she sighed.

"I hope your doctor doesn't do this to you," he murmured, running his hand up the inside of her thigh.

Marisa put her arms around his neck and drew him on top of her, locking her legs around him.

"I'm going to say something to you that I've never said to another man," she whispered, licking the shell of his ear.

"What's that?"

"Take off your clothes."

"You'll have to let me go."

"Just for a moment," she said.

He stood and stripped as she watched greedily, then dove back onto the bed, embracing her immediately.

"I think you're the most beautiful man I've ever seen," she said, arching her back as he ran a trail of kisses down her neck.

"That's not saying much. I'm the *only* man you've ever seen."

"I didn't mean naked, I mean . . . in general."

"How about, in specific?" he said thickly, guiding her hand to enclose him.

"That, too," Marisa replied, caressing him.

He groaned and pressed her back into the bed.

"Now," she said urgently.

He obeyed.

Marisa saw Jack every day until the day before court hearings began again. On the morning that the case was due to resume she wore a pink dress with a shawl collar and paired it with navy shoes and purse. She was fastening her earrings when Tracy came through the door.

"You look so nice! Ain't love grand?" she said.

"I'm discovering that it is."

"Just remember whose side you're on," Tracy said warningly.

"What's that supposed to mean?" Marisa asked, glancing at Tracy in the hotel mirror.

"Well, you might be affected by your feelings for Jack, don't you think?"

"I'm trying very hard to keep the two situations completely separate," Marisa replied.

"Good luck."

"Tracy, don't make this any more difficult for me. I'm nervous enough as it is," Marisa said, picking up her briefcase.

Tracy nodded, looking away.

"And send that file over to the clerk as soon as it's ready," Marisa added as she left.

Tracy looked after her thoughtfully.

As soon as Marisa arrived in court that day she knew that something was wrong. Jack, seated at the NFN desk, would not meet her eyes. His whole demeanor was stiff and unyielding. Ben Brady, on the other hand, looked positively exuberant. Marisa took her seat, her heart pounding, wondering desperately what was happening.

"All rise," the clerk called as Judge Lasky made his entrance.

Marisa stared at Jack as the clerk announced the case and docket number.

"Mr. Brady?" Judge Lasky said, rattling papers on the bench.

"Your honor, I would petition the court to grant a summary judgment for my client, the organization known as Natives for Nature."

Marisa stared at him, thunderstruck. What the hell was this?

Lasky raised his brows wearily. "Mr. Brady, I warn you. This had better be good."

"Your honor, this past Friday, a representative from the Bureau of Indian Affairs, Department of the Interior, a Mr. Randall Block, attempted to bribe me."

There was a stir in the courtroom. Marisa stared at Jack's back, which was ramrod straight.

Lasky banged his gavel.

"That's a serious accusation, Mr. Brady," Lasky said, when all was quiet again. "Please elucidate."

"I was offered a considerable sum of money to convince the NFN to drop this suit, so that the federal government could proceed with the highway without opposition and without delay."

"I see. There will be a short recess while I consider the situation. Counsel will approach the bench." He banged the gavel again.

The courtroom erupted into sound as Marisa, still in a state of shock, rose in obedience. She turned as she passed to look at Jack.

One glance at his stony face told her that he was convinced she was a party to the bribery attempt.

# Seven

"**M**r. Brady, were these dramatics really necessary?"
Judge Lasky said with obvious restraint to the NFN
counsel, when both lawyers were standing in front of
the bench.

"Well, your honor..." Brady began.

Lasky waved his hand dismissively. "You could have
approached me in chambers about this and handled it
quietly. But then the press would not have been racing
for the courtroom doors at this very moment, isn't that
right?"

Brady tried, and failed, to look chastised.

Lasky sighed. "Mr. Brady, it would be well for you
to remember that I am sixty-four years old and that no
matter what you try to pull, I have seen it all before,
many times. Is that clear?"

"Yes, your honor," Brady said, with as much hu-
mility as he could muster.

Lasky turned his gaze on Marisa, who was standing, dumbstruck, at Brady's side.

"Ms. Hancock, I suppose you know nothing about this charge of bribery that Mr. Brady has lodged against the representatives of the federal government?"

Marisa cleared her throat. "No, your honor."

"I was sure not," Lasky said dryly.

"I intend to investigate this incident thoroughly..." she began again, but Lasky cut her off abruptly.

"You will do nothing," Lasky said sharply. "I am declaring a recess while I locate this Mr...." He looked at Brady.

"Block," Brady supplied.

"Block," Lasky continued, "and get to the bottom of this. And I am warning you in advance, Mr. Brady, that if I discover you have fabricated any of this for the purposes of delay or confusion, your disbarment will begin to look like a very appealing prospect to me."

Brady did not look at all worried, which dismayed Marisa further; he must know he was on safe ground.

Lasky waved them away and looked up at the full court.

"This court is in recess until..." He looked at his calendar. "Thursday, December 18th, at 9:00 a.m. unless you are advised otherwise in the interim," he concluded.

The spectators rose to leave, buzzing with renewed speculation. Marisa hurried after Jack, who was already near the door.

"Jack, wait," she called.

He halted but did not turn to look at her.

Marisa ran around to confront him.

"Jack, I had nothing to do with any bribe," she said flatly, her eyes locking with his. "The first I heard of it was this morning in court."

He said nothing, but she could see that he did not believe her.

"Jack, you know me! You're not going to take the word of some federal flunky you've never met over mine?"

"I've met him," Jack said quietly.

Marisa stared at him, taken aback. Then she said, "The courtroom next door is empty. Come in there with me for a few minutes and let's talk."

He hesitated.

"Please?" she said.

He followed her reluctantly, his mouth set. Once inside, Marisa closed the double doors behind them.

"Can't you see what's happening?" Marisa began. "This guy Block was upset at the way things were going, and he misjudged Brady on the basis of what he observed. Brady is a flamboyant blowhard, true, but he's honest. Block thought he could slip him some money and Brady would then tell the NFN to drop the case. Instead it backfired and Brady blew the whistle on him. That's all there is to it."

"I've seen Block myself," Jack replied flatly. "When Brady told him he was going to Lasky with this, Block admitted that the whole thing was your idea. You knew you couldn't win in court so you thought up this clever scheme to come out on top another way."

"You don't actually believe that!" Marisa said, aghast.

"Why not? It makes sense."

"Then where is Block? Let him say this to my face. I want to see him do it!"

"I'm sure he's back in Washington, trying to salvage his career. Don't worry, Lasky will make certain he's brought in and questioned to everyone's satisfaction." Jack turned to go.

"Jack, is that all you have to say to me?" Marisa demanded, astonished.

He looked back at her. "Not quite all. You used me. I still can't believe I was quite that stupid, but apparently I was. You won't get the chance again."

"How did I use you?" Marisa asked, trying desperately to maintain her sanity.

"You pursued a relationship with me in order to gain my confidence while plotting behind my back," he said tightly. "Is that clear enough for you?"

Stinging tears filled Marisa's eyes. "Jack, how could you think that after..."

"You slept with me?" Jack finished for her. "Great little convincer, that was. And having your friend Tracy front for you, that was a nice move too."

"Front for me?" Marisa gasped.

"Yes, setting me up with touching stories about your innocence and lack of experience with men. I swallowed it all, didn't I?"

Marisa's distress was turning to anger. "Are you suggesting that I remained a virgin for twenty-eight years in order to entrap you?" she demanded icily.

"I'm suggesting you manipulated that...situation...in order to make me feel..." he stopped.

"What?" she whispered.

"In order to make me feel that you loved me!" he yelled.

"I do love you," she wailed.

"Bull!" he shouted and turned on his heel for the door.

Marisa ran after him and grabbed his arm. He wheeled and seized her shoulders so hard that she winced.

"Stay away from me," he said warningly. "I don't want to hurt you but I just might, so leave me alone." He released her suddenly and bolted through the doors before she could say anything else.

Marisa looked after him despairingly, unable to take in what had happened since she arrived at the court-house that morning.

"What are you doing back so early?" Tracy said, looking up from her pile of notes. Then her expression changed. "My God, you look ghastly. What happened?"

Marisa told her, as briefly as possible, while Tracy stared at her in appalled silence.

"I can't believe it," Tracy whispered.

"That makes two of us," Marisa said, unbuttoning her jacket, still in a state of shock.

"What are you going to do?"

"I have no idea," Marisa said miserably, wiping her eyes.

"You have to find Block, that's the first thing."

"I've already called the Bureau three times and left messages. His secretary keeps saying that he's in a meeting."

"I'll bet—what used to be called a lynching party. He never thought Brady would turn him in. I knew Block was stupid."

"And now he's trying to bail out by saying it was all my idea," Marisa replied.

"Oh, he won't get away with that. He's just buying time. You'll straighten it out in the end, you'll see."

"I'd better, or I'll be lining up at the unemployment office." Marisa sat down hard and stared at the carpet fixedly without replying.

"That's not the worst of it, is it?" Tracy murmured.

Marisa raised her eyes. "Tracy, Jack wouldn't even listen to me," she said softly.

"He's just hurt, Marisa. Once he calms down he'll think better of it and call you, I know it."

Marisa shook her head. "You weren't there, you didn't see his face." She threw up her hands. "How could he take the word of that snake from the Bureau over mine?"

"He's not in love with Block, he's in love with you."

"Oh, what does that mean?" Marisa moaned.

"It means he's proud and sensitive and taking a big chance on you, right? Even the suggestion that you might not feel the same way about him, that you might have had ulterior motives for your relationship with him, is bound to drive him wild."

"But it isn't true!"

"He'll see that, eventually."

"Easy for you to say."

"Why don't you give him a day or two to cool down and then go and see him?"

"Assuming he doesn't shoot me on sight."

"He'll calm down."

"I wish I could be sure of that. He was wild, Tracy. I've never seen him like that."

"But you knew that potential was there," Tracy replied.

Marisa looked at her.

"That's part of what attracted you to him so strongly, isn't it?" Tracy said sagely.

"I've never analyzed it," Marisa said.

"Well, I have."

"Of course."

"It's the attraction of opposites. There's a lake of fire smoldering beneath that polished surface of Jack's, and you've always known that, haven't you?"

"I didn't expect it to burn me!" Marisa protested. "He was so unreasonable. Nothing I said had the slightest impact on him."

"What did you think would happen?"

"I thought he would have some faith in me!"

"Maybe he's more insecure than he seems," Tracy observed.

Marisa snorted.

"I mean it. Look at his background, look where he comes from. He must have had some dreadful experiences while he was growing up."

"He won't talk about it much, but I think you're right."

"So there! You must seem like a goddess to him."

"Please," Marisa said disgustedly.

"Think about it. Sure, he's gorgeous. Sure, he's been around quite a bit, but has he ever had a serious relationship with somebody like you? I doubt it. Is it any wonder that he's vulnerable to the suggestion that you were manipulating him?"

"But what do I have to do to convince him otherwise? He's turned into a madman!"

"Wait it out, as I said. He'll come around. In the meantime, let's see if we can unearth Randall Block."

"And I'd better call Charlie at the firm right now and tell him what's happened," Marisa said resignedly.

"Don't you think you should alert his cardiac specialist first?" Tracy said dryly.

"If *he* thinks I was in on the bribe I'll kill myself."

"I wouldn't worry about Charlie. He's got a high-tech computer ticking away in his chest. He's never allowed an emotion to cloud his judgment in his life."

Marisa nodded and picked up the phone.

Jack shut down the word processing program in disgust and threw his notes in the trash. It was impossible to work. He couldn't think straight enough to count to ten. His manuscript would be late, his editor would go crazy, and the NFN case against the government was stalled indefinitely while Lasky tried to decide who was lying about what. His life was in a shambles, all because he was stupid enough to fall for a regal blonde with an innocent manner and a heart of stone.

He sat back in his chair and rubbed his eyes. He was not crying; his eyes were tearing from fatigue. He blinked until he had himself under control and then rose to get a drink.

In the kitchen he fumbled around for the bottle of Scotch whiskey at the back of the cabinet. When he located it he splashed several fingers of the amber liquid into a glass and drank it neat. He gasped as it hit his stomach and the fire spread through his belly. It didn't help much, but a little. Any relief was welcome.

He couldn't wait to wrap up this case and leave Florida forever. All it meant to him now was bittersweet memories he wished he could erase from his brain. It was no fun recalling what an idiot he had been, and a change of scenery might make it easier to forget. He was tempted to jump on a plane and let Brady wrap up the case alone, but that was a little too much like flight, and he was damned if he was going to run. He would face her down and show her up for the rotten little deceiver she was.

Jack looked at the bottle and then resolutely put it away. His father had been an alcoholic, and he was not heading down that road. He had been through painful episodes before and had survived. He would survive this, even though it didn't seem like it at the moment.

He couldn't forget Block's smug expression as the agent told him how Marisa had come to him with her clever plan to put an end to the NFN case. The warning signs had been there all along, of course, but Jack had been too much in love to heed them. Marisa's career was very important to her. She prided herself on her win record, and she especially wanted to beat overblown Ben Brady. She couldn't lose, that was all, and when she saw that she was going to do just that she pulled a last rabbit out of the hat to try to save the situation. And her relationship with Jack had been a ploy to keep him off-guard and maybe get some inside information while she worked the angles. He was a jerk, all right, a prize bull led to the slaughter by the delicate scent of perfume.

Jack swallowed the rest of his drink abruptly, hoping that if he got semi-sloshed he'd be able to sleep. Then he felt his way upstairs in the dark and fell into bed.

Marisa took Tracy's advice and waited three days before she went to see Jack. She didn't call first because she knew he would refuse to see her. She drove her hired car out to his isolated house just after sunset and knocked on his door with her heart banging in her chest. When he appeared seconds later she blurted out, "Don't throw me out, Jack, please give me a chance to talk to you."

Jack studied her for a long moment in silence and then stepped aside, allowing her to precede him into the house.

"I really don't think we have anything more to say to each other," he said neutrally.

"How can you just dismiss me?" she demanded. "Isn't there any chance I could be telling the truth?"

"No," he said flatly.

"Why?" Marisa countered, trying very hard to stay calm.

"I knew you were too good to be true, and I was right. I just wish I had realized it before I made a fool of myself."

"It's very important for you to hurt me now, isn't it?" she said quietly.

"Why not? Turnabout is fair play."

"You never believed I loved you, did you?" she said miserably.

"I believe you wanted to sleep with me, even you are not that good an actress. As an amusement, I'm sure I was satisfactory. I've never had any complaints in that direction. And all that business about keeping the relationship going after the case was over, that was just a red herring to throw me off the track. Can't have the pigeon catching on before the trap is sprung, right?"

"Once I get Randall Block into court I'll force him to tell the truth, and then you'll see," she said desperately.

"Save your breath. He's already telling the truth."

"He got a federal judge to issue a restraining order against me," Marisa said.

"Smart guy."

"He knew he could dodge my calls only so long before I showed up in person."

"Terrifying prospect. What were you going to do, bludgeon him with your briefcase?" he said sarcastically.

"I don't know," Marisa said in a small voice.

"Why don't you try sleeping with him? That seems to work very well for you."

Marisa gasped, staring at him, unable to reply.

"Maybe you could try the virgin routine with him, too. No, I guess that only works once. Well, you're an inventive lady, never fear, you'll think of something."

"You louse," Marisa whispered.

"That makes two of us. Will there be anything else?" He motioned toward the door.

"Yes," Marisa said hoarsely. "I have something else to say."

"Make it quick."

"You are going to regret this," she began.

"I doubt it."

"Oh, I know you doubt it now, but you will remember this day and the things you said to me and realize what a mistake you made."

He glared back at her stonily.

"I'm the best thing that ever happened to you, and you're throwing me away because you're so insecure and cynical and just plain stupid...."

"Watch it," he said tightly.

"What are you going to do, big man?" she said, fighting tears. "Punch me, the way you punched that kid at the Seminole gallery? That's your standard method of solving problems, isn't it?"

"Get the hell out of here."

"I've done nothing wrong!" Marisa burst out, suddenly overwhelmed by the unfairness of it. "I didn't attempt to bribe anybody. I knew nothing about what Block was doing until I heard about it in court. But if this is what it took to show me what a narrow, limited, prejudiced person you really are..."

"Prejudiced!" he said disbelievingly.

"You heard me," Marisa said, crying openly now. "You think I'm just like that girlfriend you had when you were in high school, too Waspy, too white bread..."

"I think that you're a liar," he said tonelessly. "They come in all colors."

"Fine," she said, throwing up her hands. "I'm leaving."

"Good."

"I'll never forget you," she sobbed, running headlong for the front door.

"I'll try to forget you," he called after her.

Marisa burst out onto the porch, blinded by tears. She dashed to the car and sat on the front seat for a couple of minutes, waiting for her vision to clear, watching the door through a mist to see if Jack would come after her.

When he didn't, she drove back to her hotel in town and went straight to bed.

"What's this?" Tracy asked, when she came in from shopping an hour later and found Marisa already huddled under the covers, clutching a box of tissues.

"It's over," Marisa said.

"What's over?"

"The World's Fair, what do you think? I took your advice and went to see Jack tonight. He was the same as before—a stone wall. Worse. He was mean and nasty and insulting and . . . I give up," she said, dissolving into tears again.

Tracy dropped her bags on the floor and sat down.

"Maybe it was too soon," she said lamely.

"Will you please stop making excuses for him?" Marisa said in irritation, pausing to blow her nose.

"He'll find out eventually that you didn't know what Block was going to do," Tracy said reasonably.

"What does that matter? This episode has shown me what he really thinks of me, and that isn't good."

"When you see him in court again . . ." Tracy began.

"I doubt we'll be going back to court," Marisa interrupted, tossing a wadded tissue into the trash bin next to the bed.

"Why not?"

"Lasky will probably declare a mistrial, and the feds will tell me to fold my tent and go home."

"And leave the cemetery to the Seminoles."

"Which is what they should have done in the first place," Marisa concluded.

"So it looks like we'll be out of here in short order," Tracy said, measuring Marisa with a glance.

"If it goes the way I think it will," Marisa replied, sniffling and rubbing her reddened nose.

"Can't be soon enough for you, I guess," Tracy said darkly.

"You got that right."

Tracy sighed. "Are you sure Charlie won't blame this debacle on us once we get back home?" she asked.

"Charlie knows what happened. And if I have to track Randall Block to the limits of civilization as we know it, he will clear this up before he dies, or I do."

"What does Charlie want you to do?"

"Nothing. Charlie's main concern is getting the feds to pay up speedily. Losing clients are notoriously less happy about paying their bills than winning clients."

"So Charlie thinks it will be over soon, too."

"Unless a new world order is established while we sleep and we wake up tomorrow with Randall Block as President."

"Now there's a thought to fill your heart with joy."

Marisa closed her eyes. "I wish I had never come here," she said plaintively.

"So we'll be back home and you can forget it."

"I can never forget it," Marisa whispered.

"The pain will fade with time. It always does."

"I'll never meet anybody else like him, Tracy. I know I'll miss him for the rest of my life."

"You're young. You'll meet somebody else."

Marisa closed her eyes. "Please don't say things like that. You sound like you're comforting me about not being asked to the senior prom."

"I didn't mean to trivialize it. I know you're hurting. I just don't know what to do to make you feel better."

"There's nothing to do." Marisa got up and set the box of tissues firmly on the nightstand. "And I am through feeling sorry for myself. I have to resurrect my career from the ashes of this nightmare, and that's going to be my priority from this moment."

"Glad to hear it," Tracy said, brightening.

"And now I'm going to take a very long, very hot, shower," Marisa announced, marching toward the bathroom.

"I'm glad to hear that, too," Tracy added, grinning.

Marisa threw her a dirty look over her shoulder.

"Well, water could only cause an improvement," Tracy said, shrugging.

Marisa pushed open the bathroom door and glanced in the mirror. "I see what you mean," she said glumly.

"I'll order dinner in the room," Tracy went on, cheering up, as usual, at the prospect of food.

"I couldn't eat anything," Marisa said, turning on the taps.

"Chicken Marsala?" Tracy suggested.

"Oh, God," Marisa whispered, leaning against the tiled wall, her gorge rising at the thought of wine sauce.

"All right," Tracy said, peeking in the door as steam billowed out of the shower stall. "Bad idea. But you can't keep on starving yourself. You're losing weight already and you can't spare it. How about a grilled cheese sandwich?"

"Yes, Mother," Marisa said, smiling weakly.

"And a glass of milk," Tracy added, as Marisa shut the door firmly in her face.

Marisa stepped under the streaming water and picked up the bar of soap, wishing that she could wash away her troubles as easily as she washed her hair.

It happened as Marisa had predicted. Judge Lasky declared a mistrial and the Indians kept their land. Marisa was recalled to Maine where she was kept very busy filing papers to answer collusion charges on the attempted bribery. She was placed on suspension and reduced to the status of law clerk while the state bar association awaited the outcome before instituting disbarment proceedings against her. She was miserable, but she had to bide her time until she was able to show that Block was lying.

About two weeks after Marisa left Florida, Jack flew to Washington and entered the familiar building which housed the Bureau of Indian Affairs. He went up in the elevator and strolled down a corridor lined with offices, looking for a particular cubicle. When he found it he looked up and down the hall to make sure that no one else was around, and then he entered quickly, startling the room's occupant.

"Hi, Randall," Jack said briskly. "Remember me?"

Block dropped his pencil.

"We're going to have another little talk," Jack announced, and kicked the door shut behind him.

# Eight

Marisa peered out the window of her house in Maine and gauged the accumulation of snow on the ground. It was enough to cause trouble but not enough to bring traffic to a standstill. She would be able to make it in to work.

She switched on the radio in the kitchen and was rewarded with the blaring sound of "Deck the Halls," reminding her that it was Christmas Eve. She turned the knob abruptly, cutting off the sound. She had never felt less festive in her life.

The coffeepot was disassembled on the drain board, and as she put the pieces together and fitted the filter into the cup she tried to remember whether she had sent her gray wool skirt to the cleaners. The navy shirt-waist was probably clean, but there was a button missing from one of the sleeves.

She sighed. She would wear whatever was easiest. She didn't have the heart, or the interest, for a wardrobe analysis. She plugged in the pot and wandered over to the front door to see if the paperboy had left the morning edition on the porch.

A blast of wintry air greeted her as she opened the door. Icicles were hanging from the eaves and Mr. Henderson across the street was already clearing his property with a roaring snowblower. Marisa regretted not pulling her car into the garage the night before; now she would have to scrape the frost off its windows.

Marisa looked in the direction of the driveway and froze. There was an object planted in a shallow drift just beyond her porch. Shielding her eyes against the glare, she saw that it was an arrow, decked out with colorful feathers.

Her heart beating faster, Marisa glanced around quickly and saw Jack leaning against her car in the driveway. Arms folded, ankles crossed, he was watching her steadily, his only concession to the weather a red woolen muffler wrapped around his throat and stuffed into the collar of his fringed jacket.

Marisa's hands went to her sleep-disordered hair and the collar of her plaid wool robe. The man did have a knack for catching her in disarray. Even so, she had to restrain herself from running barefoot across the frozen lawn and into his arms. Then she remembered how angry she was with him and forced herself to remain where she was.

Jack sauntered toward Marisa as she stood planted like a tree on her front steps, too amazed to move. Then he stopped a few feet away from her and held out a manila envelope.

"What's this?" she asked flatly, looking at it intently, then back at his face.

"Please take it," he said.

After a second, she did.

"Open it," he said.

"Jack, I'm not in any mood for games. You'd better tell me what's inside."

"It's a full confession from Randall Block, taking sole responsibility for the attempted bribe and clearing you completely."

Marisa exhaled a long, slow breath, studying Jack's intent expression. Then she flung the envelope in his face, whirled, and slammed the door behind her.

"Marisa, open up!" Jack shouted, pounding on the door. "Come on, this isn't fair!"

"Fair!" she yelled back at him through the solid oak door, shooting the deadbolt home with a flick of her wrist. "Who are you to talk to me about fair? Go back to Florida!"

"I came from Oklahoma."

"Then go back there. Just leave me alone."

"Marisa, please. Can't you listen for a minute?"

"Just like you listened to me? I remember how patient and understanding you were about Block's accusations. How dare you show up here with that thing in your hand and expect me to forget your inexcusable behavior?"

"I don't expect that. I just want to talk to you."

Marisa hesitated.

"Marisa, it's Christmas. Are you going to leave me out here on the lawn, peering in the window like the Little Match Girl?"

Marisa sighed heavily.

"I will let you in," she called, "but once you've said your piece I expect you to leave without any further discussion."

There was a profound, extended silence from the other side of the door.

"Well?" Marisa demanded.

"I don't suppose I have any choice," Jack replied.

Marisa opened the door cautiously. Jack was waiting with his arms behind his back, his expression wary.

"Come in," she said, belting her robe tighter around her waist. He stepped past her, looking around her living room curiously.

"Great old house," he commented and deposited the arrow he'd left on her lawn on the entry hall table.

"Did you come here to discuss New England architecture?" Marisa asked frostily.

"You're not going to give me a break, I see," he said.

"Do you think I should?" she countered.

He thrust the envelope back into her hands. "Just read it, will you please?"

Marisa broke the seal with her fingernail and removed the two sheets of typewritten paper. She read them through quickly and then looked up at Jack.

"How did you get this?" she asked.

"Randall and I had a little talk."

"What does that mean? You beat him up?"

"I...encouraged him to be truthful," Jack said flatly.

"I would have bought a ticket to that," Marisa said dryly, thumbing her hair behind her ears.

"Does that mean I get a cup of coffee?" he asked, sniffing the aroma that was drifting in from the kitchen.

"All right. One cup, and then you go." She marched into the kitchen and he trailed after her, looking around at the family pictures on the walls in the hall.

"You were a cute kid," he observed.

Marisa got a mug from the cupboard, filled it with coffee, and handed it to him.

"Are you going to watch and time me while I drink it?" he asked defensively.

Marisa indicated the wall clock. "I have to be at work at eight-thirty," she said pointedly.

He sat the mug on the counter resignedly. "Aren't you even going to thank me for getting Block's confession? It's already on its way to the Justice Department."

Marisa stared at him stonily. "Thank you."

He sighed. "This isn't going the way I planned. When I showed you that confession you were supposed to scream for joy and throw yourself into my arms."

"I haven't forgotten your behavior when you first heard Block's lies," she replied.

Jack looked at the floor. "Marisa, I'm sorry."

"I accept your apology. Now you can go."

He looked up. "Don't I even get a chance to explain why I acted the way I did?"

"I know why. You have no faith in me."

"I have no faith in *me*," he said quietly.

"Jack . . ."

"Yeah, I know. You have to go to work." He took a breath, then said, "Can I see you for dinner?"

"I don't think that would be such a good idea."

"You really do want to punish me, don't you, Marisa?" he said miserably.

"I just can't take any more, Jack. I've had enough. I want my life to go back to the way it was before I met you. Maybe it was dull, but it wasn't painful."

"Wouldn't you have dinner with any friend who came to town and wanted to see you?"

"We're not friends."

"We're lovers," he said softly.

"Were," Marisa said quietly. "We were lovers."

Jack nodded. "Okay. I'll tell you what. I'll call on you tonight and see how you're feeling then."

"I'll probably be feeling the same."

"Tough as nails, aren't you?"

"If I am, you made me that way." She looked at the clock significantly again.

"I'm going," he said.

Marisa escorted him through the hall. "Goodbye, Jack," she said evenly.

He looked at her for a long moment, then walked through the door. Once it was closed behind him, Marisa sagged against the wall and burst into tears.

She was cleared, and Jack was here. It was all too much to take in at once, and the extreme restraint she had exercised while he was with her gave way to a storm of weeping that left her feeling exhausted.

She hadn't even asked why he had arrived at dawn or where he was staying. All she could think of was getting rid of him before she collapsed into his arms. She mustn't forget that there was a serious problem with their relationship, or he wouldn't have treated her the way he had. To pretend that it hadn't happened would be a mistake.

But she had to admit that she was already looking forward to seeing him that night.

* * *

The firm closed at noon for the annual Christmas party. Marisa had handed Charlie Wellman her copy of Block's confession as soon as she got to work that day, so there was more than the Yuletide to celebrate. When Tracy showed up after her last class with a wrapped package, she found Marisa still in her office, on the phone.

Tracy, dressed in a red suit and wearing an elf's hat, waved frantically from the doorway.

"Okay, I'll send you a hard copy of that first thing after the holiday," Marisa said into the phone. She listened for a second, said, "Right, goodbye, and Merry Christmas," and hung up the phone.

"Fa la la la la," Tracy said. "I hate to tell you this, but there's a party going on out there. You're the only one still working." She waltzed into the room and planted the gift on Marisa's desk blotter.

"You've got the spirit," Marisa said.

"Sandy Carter asked me to the New Year's Eve dance at the Eaglesmere Country Club," Tracy confided, chuckling wickedly.

"Congratulations. I have a little bulletin myself."

"What?" Tracy flicked a tinkling bell on one of the Christmas wall decorations with her fingernail.

"Jack is here."

"Where?" Tracy glanced around wildly as if she expected to find him stashed in a corner of the room.

"He came to my house first thing this morning. And guess what he gave me?"

Tracy sat in Marisa's client chair. "I'm all ears."

Marisa told Tracy everything that had happened at her house that day. When she finished Tracy asked excitedly, "What are you going to do tonight?"

"I don't know."

"Well, he's coming back, isn't he?"

"He said so."

"Don't look at me," Tracy said, waving her hand. "I would throw myself into his arms and drag him off to bed, so I'm a bad one to give advice."

"I have to be sensible."

"Oh, please. You're always sensible. Try reckless for once, it just might work."

"I was reckless enough back in Florida for ten people."

"And wound up with this gorgeous man madly in love with you. Big mistake, huh?"

The door to the hall opened, admitting the sound of "Jingle Bell Rock" and party merriment into the room.

"What are you two doing in here?" Charlie demanded. "Mark Dempsey is dancing with the dermatologist from the fifth floor and Judge Jerrold is about to do the limbo under Sadie's mop handle."

"Wouldn't want to miss that," Tracy observed dryly.

"Be right with you, Charlie," Marisa said.

"I should imagine that you'd be in a celebrating mood," Charlie said to Marisa and winked, pulling the door closed behind him.

"I think he's drunk," Tracy said

Marisa reached for the gift box on her desk. "I sent your present to your house," she said, tearing into the wrapping.

"A complete set of the *Encyclopaedia Britannica*, I trust?" Tracy said brightly.

"Nothing so educational."

"Goody."

Marisa tore off the last of the silver paper impatiently and gasped with delight.

"Indigo Sky!" she exclaimed, unscrewing the crystal stopper of a tiny bottle of her favorite perfume.

"It's only toilet water, a minuscule amount at that, it's all I could afford. But I know how much you like it."

"How thoughtful," Marisa murmured, touched.

"Now get out of here and go home to that wonderful man," Tracy said, rising.

"I should go out to the party and mix a little."

"Oh, forget about that. I'll make your excuses and mix enough for both of us. Get going."

Marisa took her coat from the hook behind her door and followed Tracy's advice.

As soon as Marisa pulled into her driveway she knew that something was up. All the lights were on in the house and there was a strange car parked in the slush by the curb. When she got out cautiously she saw Jack appear in the front window, then come to the door.

"What are you doing in here?" Marisa demanded.

"That ancient lock you've got on your door wouldn't keep out a clever four-year-old," he answered briskly, stepping aside to admit her to her own house. He was wearing tailored dark slacks and a cream wool pullover that made his dark eyes and hair vivid in the softly lit room.

Marisa stopped and stared in surprise. A completely decorated tree stood next to the fireplace, where a cheerful fire was burning. The coffee table was set with two of her mother's crystal glasses and a bottle of champagne on ice, and the enticing smell of a cooking roast drifted in from the direction of the kitchen.

"Did you do all this?" she asked in wonderment.

"Nobody else."

"That fireplace doesn't work," she said, walking up to it and peering closely at the flames.

"It does now. The flue was stuck. I fixed it."

"And where did you get that tree?"

"Finley's Department Store. Christmas Eve special, fully decorated, half price."

"I see. And you've learned to cook, too?"

"Speedy Gourmet on Tenth Street. You can buy anything you want already prepared, all you have to do is heat it up."

"Amazing. You must have gone through town like a tornado. And the wine? Let me guess. Lake Country Liquors."

"Right the first time."

Marisa dropped her briefcase and purse on a chair. "What is all this in aid of, Jack? I mean, it's very nice and everything . . ."

"It's Christmas, Marisa," he said quietly. "Can't you relax a little and give me a break?"

"What do you want?" she said flatly.

"Another chance," he said simply. "I love you. I'm sorry for what I did, and I want another chance."

Marisa sat in her grandfather's old easy chair near the fire. "We didn't have a little spat, Jack. You took someone else's word over mine on an important issue, and when I begged you to listen to me you simply wouldn't do it. You insulted me and . . ."

"Please don't remind me of my asinine behavior," he interrupted miserably.

"What I'm saying is . . ."

"I know what you're saying. You think it wasn't an isolated incident and things like that will keep happening again and again."

"Will you kindly stop interrupting me?"

He sat across from her on the sofa and folded his arms, his expression bleak.

"You really hurt me, Jack."

He turned his head, looking away from her.

"I know," he said, very quietly.

"What made you change your mind finally and go to see Randall Block?"

He sighed. "After you left Florida I had a chance to calm down and think things over, and I just couldn't believe that you had resorted to bribery."

"Gee, it seems to me that I tried to tell you the same thing," Marisa said lightly. "More than once."

"Spare me the sarcasm, Marisa, this is hard enough as it is," Jack said wearily.

"Go on," she said.

"So I tracked Block back to Washington and had a discussion with him."

"I see. Has he been discharged from the hospital yet?" Marisa asked pointedly.

"I didn't harm him. I wanted him to be in perfect health to testify about his actions."

"So how did you threaten him?"

"What does it matter? I got him to tell the truth, and that's what counts."

"You should have known I would never do such a thing. If you really loved me you wouldn't have credited that stupid story for a minute," Marisa responded, the old anger surging inside her again.

The both looked up as the sound of singing outside became audible and then came gradually closer, reaching a crescendo just outside the front door.

"Carolers," Marisa said. "I have some cookies in the kitchen."

She went to get the tray and came back into the living room, opening the door and distributing the treats to the children on the porch. Jack watched as she chatted with them and they rewarded her with a shaky version of "Silent Night."

"You seem to know all of them," he commented, as she closed the door behind the departing group.

"It's a small town. I went to grade school with some of their parents."

"You must think about having children of your own," he said.

"Sometimes."

"Want to get started on it tonight?" he asked.

Marisa resumed her seat and glared at him.

"Okay, bad joke. Where were we?"

"I believe I was saying that if you really loved me you would never have listened to Block's lies in the first place."

"I was hoping you'd skip over that part."

"I think I deserve an explanation," Marisa persisted, her tone as firm as her gaze.

"It's complicated."

"Oh, it must be."

He strode over to the fireplace and leaned on the mantel. "I've always found it difficult to trust 'the suits,' you know, people like you, establishment types."

"Thank you."

"You know what I mean. You come from this tin-type town, you have education and background on your side, you were representing the government in this case, you came straight from the places I had never fit into in my whole life."

"Next we'll be tracing my bloodlines back to good Queen Bess," Marisa observed to the air.

He closed his eyes. "I found it difficult to accept that a sophisticated woman like you would want me. It was easier to think that you were using me."

"You mean that despite your success you feel inside that you're still back on the reservation."

His eyes opened and met hers.

"Yes," he said flatly.

"I've already gathered that much, Jack. You can't use that as an excuse for treating me so badly."

"Marisa, when it seemed you had manipulated me it just played right into a whole lifetime of doubt and suspicion."

Marisa was silent.

"All right, so I've never been in love before and I don't know how to act!" he said heatedly.

"What do you mean, you've never been in love before?" Marisa demanded.

"Just what I said. It's not a difficult concept." He sat next to her on the sofa and she inched backward.

"Will you stop doing that?" he said in exasperation.

"What?"

"Every time I come near you a silent alarm goes off and you put distance between us."

"I'm trying to think clearly."

"And you can't think clearly when I touch you?"

"Right."

"Doesn't that tell you something?"

"It tells me that you're trying to confuse me!" she said, almost in tears, rising and going to the window.

He followed, standing just behind her and looking out at the silently falling snow.

"Nobody will ever love you as much as I do," he said softly, touching her shoulder.

"I know that," she whispered.

"Nobody will ever be as good for you as I am," he added.

She nodded.

"Then why not give me another chance?" he said.

She turned blindly into his arms.

"You hurt me so badly," she sobbed.

"I know, and I'm so sorry. I'll try to be better in the future." He held her tightly, his lips moving in her hair.

"I thought you would never come around. I thought I had lost you forever," she went on.

"I felt like a prize jerk once I got the truth out of Block. I came here as quickly as I could," he murmured.

"Just hold me. I missed you so."

They stood together for a long moment, and then he led her by the hand back to the sofa.

"I have something for you," he said, sitting next to her again, closer this time.

"Something else?" she said.

He withdrew a small square box from his pants pocket and placed it in her hand.

Marisa looked up at him.

"Open it."

Marisa sprung the catch. An emerald cut diamond set in gleaming white gold sparkled against a bed of deep blue velvet.

"Where did you get this?" she gasped.

"Faber's Jewelers, corner of Main and Grand."

"Not from Mr. Faber!"

"It wouldn't surprise me. Old guy about seventy, on the short side, thinning white hair, eastern European accent?"

"You didn't tell him it was for me," Marisa groaned.

"Sure, why not?"

"Mr. Faber was my grandfather's poker buddy, not to mention that they grew up together, practically slept in the same bassinet. He's the worst gossip in the town, in the world. Everybody will know by tomorrow morning."

"Good. Then you'll have to marry me."

"Jack..."

"Yes?"

"I'll marry you."

He pulled her into his arms almost roughly, knocking the ring box on the floor.

"I have to ask you a question," he said in her ear.

"What?"

"Have you got any money?"

She drew back to look at him.

"I exhausted my credit card limit buying that ring," he said, laughing helplessly.

"I have twenty-three dollars in my purse," she said.

"That will have to last until day after tomorrow."

The scent of burning food wafted down the hall.

"There goes dinner," Jack said.

"I have some tuna in the pantry." She disentangled herself from his arms and stood, straightening her clothes. "Let me go turn off the oven and I'll see if I can put together a casserole..."

"Turn off the oven and then come to the bedroom," he said quietly. "Where is it?"

"Right at the end of the hall," Marisa said. She went to the kitchen and fumbled with the knob on the stove, her fingers trembling. Then she made a feeble pass at straightening her hair as she followed Jack into the bedroom.

He was waiting and handed her a glass of champagne.

"To us," he said, toasting her.

"To us," she repeated.

They touched glasses and drank. Then he put his down and took her glass from her hand.

"Now come here," he said.

She was only too happy to obey.

# Epilogue

"So now I have to start planning a baby shower?" Tracy said. "I haven't recovered from the wedding yet."

"It's not definite," Marisa replied, pouring coffee into Tracy's cup. "I haven't seen a doctor."

They were sitting in Marisa's kitchen on a Saturday morning in late March, with the first spring thaw melting the icicles on the roofline outside the window.

"Didn't you take one of those home tests?"

"Yes, but they're not always accurate."

"Come on. Was it positive?"

Marisa grinned.

"You didn't have to say it," Tracy said, smiling conspiratorially. "You've got the glow."

"I've got the nausea, I can tell you that. I can't contemplate food until about three in the afternoon."

"You must be so excited."

"I think I'm just in a daze. If anyone had told me when I left Florida that three months later I would be married to Jack, and pregnant, I would have laughed. Derisively."

"Have you told Jack?"

Marisa shook her head. "I just found out this morning, and I didn't want to tell him over the phone."

"When is he due back from his trip?"

"About eight."

"Big doings tonight, then. What will you say? How are you going to tell him?"

"Well, once he starts seeing me turn green at the sight of his breakfast, he'll know. He's been in Japan for two weeks promoting *Renegade*."

"Is that his new book?"

Marisa nodded, taking a sip of her milk. "A thinly disguised account of our romance, I'm afraid. He was already writing it during the trial in Florida. Do you believe that?"

Tracy giggled. "You're kidding."

"Nope. His hero, Roger Whitemoon, falls for a lady lawyer, a New Englander who goes up against him in a complicated legal case. Sound familiar?"

"Am I in it?" Tracy asked eagerly.

"Well, the lady lawyer has a pal named Cindy who works as her researcher."

"A beautiful, seductive, brilliant pal named Cindy," Tracy corrected archly.

"Of course."

"Who is responsible for bringing the lovers together in an act of friendship and generosity unparalleled in human history."

"Right."

"I still can't get used to having Jack here all the time. Has he sold his condo in Oklahoma yet?"

"The real estate agent thinks she has a buyer, but she isn't sure if he'll qualify for the mortgage," Marisa said.

"I don't think this town has recovered yet from the idea of Jack as a full-time resident. Did you see the ad Mr. Faber ran in the newspaper, describing the ring Jack bought for you in his store?"

"You mean 'Come to Faber's, Jeweler to the Rich and Famous?'" Marisa asked, closing her eyes.

"That's the one," Tracy responded, cackling.

"Mr. Faber has never been known to pass up a lucrative business opportunity."

"I think everybody in this town is secretly disappointed that you haven't razed this tired old place and erected some sort of palace in its stead."

"Jack really isn't the palace type, and neither am I. We did buy the house in Florida, though. For sentimental reasons. And I've ordered vinyl siding to be put on here in May."

"My, you are getting frivolous. What next? A new fence? Painting the shutters? The neighbors *will* be talking."

"What were they expecting, for heaven's sake?"

"Well, you know how it is. A bestselling author moving into a seventy-year-old Cape Cod is not their idea of a luxurious life-style. At the very least, Jack should be driving some expensive Italian sports car, that 4 × 4 of his just doesn't cut it."

"But he's from out West. There are mountains and foothills and the terrain is rough. A vehicle like that is practical."

Tracy stared at her.

"I'm sorry we're so dull," Marisa said, sighing.

"But not in the bedroom. I'm sure you're not dull in the bedroom," Tracy observed wickedly.

Marisa threw a napkin at her.

"I suppose Jack could do a rain dance on the front lawn," Tracy suggested. "At least that would satisfy their curiosity about his Indian background."

"I'll mention it to him."

"And now I have to go," Tracy said, rising. "I have a paper due next week that's still in the note-card stage."

"Okay. Good luck with the work."

"Give my best to Jack. And to junior in there." She patted Marisa's tummy.

"I will."

"I'll see you at the office on Monday morning." Tracy sailed out the back door.

Marisa put their dishes in the sink, feeling once more the secret elation that had become part of her inner life ever since she realized that she was pregnant. Jack would be so thrilled. She was preparing a special dinner, all of his favorites, but if she knew her man they would be in bed before they had a chance to eat it. She was getting very good at wrapping leftovers.

Marisa went to get her doctor's office number to make an appointment.

Jack swept through the door at eight-ten, carrying a stack of parcels and drenched with a cold rain. Marisa was waiting for him in the living room, sitting next to the roaring fire and holding a glass of his special Napoleon brandy.

"Woman!" he shouted and threw the boxes on a chair.

Marisa put down the drink and ran into his arms.

"Oh, God, you feel so warm and good," he murmured, his mouth moving in her hair. "I missed you terribly. Why the hell didn't you come with me anyway?"

"Jack, we discussed it before you left. I had that case going before the Superior Court and..."

"Never mind," he said, holding her off to look at her. "I'm back now. Is it possible that you got more gorgeous while I was gone?"

"Jack, you were gone two weeks," she said, laughing and smoothing his wet hair.

"Two weeks prettier, no doubt about it," he said and kissed her lingeringly, his face wet with rain.

"Jack..." Marisa whispered.

"What?" he replied distractedly, steering her firmly toward the bedroom.

"Don't you want your drink?"

"Not as much as I want you."

"Wait a minute...." she said, as he started to unbutton her blouse.

"Yes?" he said innocently.

"Jack," she said, more urgently.

He slid his hand up her back to unhook her bra.

"Jack!" she protested.

"Yes?" he said again, grinning.

"What did you bring me?"

He burst out laughing. "You really don't want me to answer that question."

"I meant, what's all that stuff in the boxes?" Marisa amended, blushing.

"Later," he said, pushing her blouse off her shoulders impatiently, his fingers chilly against her skin.

Marisa closed her eyes.

Jack trailed his tongue across her collarbone and down into the valley between her breasts.

Marisa sighed. "Later," she agreed.

They hit the bed hard and did not resume the conversation until some time later. Marisa was propped against Jack's shoulder, thinking how perfectly and utterly happy she was, when she said drowsily, "So how was Japan?"

Jack chuckled softly. "Lonely."

"I'll bet. Did you meet any geishas?"

He kissed the top of her head. "Counselor, it's clear you've never been on a book junket."

"True."

"Even if I'd had any desire to expand my horizons in that direction, I was too busy to do it."

"Hmmpf," she said disbelievingly.

"It's true. Publishing houses do not sponsor these trips for authors to visit the tourist attractions. They expect you to flog the book twenty-four hours a day."

"And did you? Flog the book?"

"Relentlessly."

"Good. You had quite a few messages from the NFN while you were gone. They want you to appear at a rally to raise money for Jeff Rivertree's legal defense."

"Okay. I'll get to them in the morning." He tightened his arm around her. "Tonight is for us."

"May I see my presents now?"

He sighed. "You're like a six-year-old."

"Come on, I'm curious." She slipped out of the bed and into a robe, padding barefoot into the living room. Jack followed, pushing back his still damp hair.

"I should warn you, they're not all for you," he said, dropping onto the sofa and taking a deep swallow of the drink Marisa had gotten for him earlier.

"What!" she said, feigning disappointment.

"I got something for my mother and Ana," he said, leaning forward to remove those boxes from the pile.

"That's permitted."

"Thank you."

Marisa tore into the first package, discarding the wrapping and lifting the lid.

"Sorry about the makeshift packaging. I had to have them wrapped after customs and . . ."

"Jack!" Marisa cried in delight, lifting a royal blue robe of heavy fugi silk from the box and holding it aloft. Emblazoned across the back of it was a golden imperial dragon, and it was encrusted with sapphire bugle beads at the collar and cuffs. The dragon's head swirled down one arm and the tail trailed down the other, the gilt embroidery contrasting sharply with the smooth silk.

"This is gorgeous," she breathed.

"I'm glad you like it," he said. "It's really for me."

Marisa looked at him.

"Just kidding," he said.

Marisa stood, dropping her tired chenille robe to the floor and then wrapping herself in the satiny folds.

"How do I look?" she said, striking a pose.

"Like the first blond empress of Japan," he said, saluting her with his glass.

"Too bad I can only wear this at home," Marisa said sadly, fingering the lapels.

"I don't recommend wearing it to the office. Charlie Wellman will have a stroke."

Marisa grinned.

Jack took another sip of his drink and added, "Open that small one next."

Marisa tore into the wrappings greedily and came up with a jeweler's box.

"You're spoiling me," she said, opening it.

"I'm trying."

"Pearls," she said, lifting a string of perfectly matched lustrous gems from the bed of cotton wool.

"I thought that necklace would match your earrings pretty well," he said.

"Oh, it does, thank you, thank you so much," she said, running to embrace him.

"Hey, hey, you're not finished yet," he protested, disentangling her arms from his neck. "There's another one."

Marisa glanced over her shoulder at the last package, discarded on the floor.

"Dinner's been warming in the oven. I should take it out before it ossifies," Marisa protested.

"It can wait a minute. Open that."

Marisa knelt obediently and opened the last package. Marisa lifted it, puzzled at first.

"What?" she said.

"Look at it closely," Jack advised.

Comprehension dawned.

"This is an Indian baby board," she said, examining the flat back and front bundling used to hold a papoose.

"Right."

"You didn't get this in Japan."

"Right again. It's Blackfoot, my mother sent it. I picked it up on the porch on the way in. It must have been left by the parcel service earlier today."

"You knew it was coming."

"I had an idea."

"Is this a family heirloom?"

He nodded.

"Am I jumping to wild conclusions, or is this a hint?"

"That's my mother, world famous for her subtlety."

Marisa put the carrier on the floor and walked over to sit next to Jack, slipping her arms around his neck.

"Jack?"

"Uh-huh?"

"I have something to tell you."

\* \* \* \* \*

# Take 4 bestselling love stories FREE

## Plus get a FREE surprise gift!

**Silhouette**
**Christmas Stories 1992**

Experience the beauty of Yuletide romance with Silhouette Christmas Stories 1992—a collection of heartwarming stories by favorite Silhouette authors.

JONI'S MAGIC by Mary Lynn Baxter
HEARTS OF HOPE by Sondra Stanford
THE NIGHT SANTA CLAUS RETURNED by Marie Ferrarella
BASKET OF LOVE by Jeanne Stephens

Also available this year are three popular early editions of Silhouette Christmas Stories—1986, 1987 and 1988. Look for these and you'll be well on your way to a complete collection of the best in holiday romance.

Plus, as an added bonus, you can receive a FREE keepsake Christmas ornament. Just collect four proofs of purchase from any November or December 1992 Harlequin or Silhouette series novels, or from any Harlequin or Silhouette Christmas collection, and receive a beautiful dated brass Christmas candle ornament.

---

Mail this certificate along with four (4) proof-of-purchase coupons, plus $1.50 postage and handling (check or money order—do not send cash), payable to Silhouette Books, to: **In the U.S.:** P.O. Box 9057, Buffalo, NY 14269-9057; **In Canada:** P.O. Box 622, Fort Erie, Ontario, L2A 5X3.

---

| ONE PROOF OF PURCHASE | Name: _____ |
| --- | --- |
| | _____ |
| | Address: _____ |
| | _____ |
| | City: _____ |
| | State/Province: _____ |
| SX92POP | Zip/Postal Code: _____ |

093 KAG